KILL CODE

KILL CODE

A Dystopian Science Fiction Novel

CLIVE FLEURY

TCK PUBLISHING.COM

ISBN: 978-1-63161-056-1

Published by TCK Publishing
www.TCKpublishing.com

Get discounts and special deals on books at
www.TCKpublishing.com/bookdeals

Get in touch with Clive and find out more at
www.clivefleurywriter.com

CHAPTER ONE

T HE VIEW OUT OF THE Dunkin' Donuts window was spectacular. The store, nestled on the clifftop, looked directly over the angry, crashing waves of the Pacific Ocean. Years ago, Dunkin' used to be a distance from the sea, but over the years, the rocks had crumbled and fallen, bringing it ever-closer to the foaming blue water.

I can still remember when Santa Monica actually had a beach. I kept old photos from back then, when the city still looked idyllic. People used to worship the sun instead of hating it. That was before the luxury high-rise apartments and hotels that lined the seafront had all been abandoned and the Pacific Coast Highway had disappeared underwater.

I collected a packet of sugar for my partner Max's breakfast coffee. As I walked back to the counter, I made a mental note to check the sea level at the end of Colorado Avenue. It seemed to be unusually high that day. Of course, the politicians always boasted that they'd gotten the flooding under control, but no one ever believed them—and, as cops, we'd been told to report any areas showing signs of unusual water rises.

The waiter put the tray of donuts and coffee down. His nametag said *Gordy*. He was a round-faced, bushy-browed teenager. Jobs like these used to be looked down upon, but with the economy continuing to freefall and the cost of education going up and up, most young kids today would kill for a job at Dunkin'. So Gordy was one of the lucky ones.

I picked up the tray and headed for the door. Since I'd been on my diet, I'd been trying to wean myself off my addiction to sweet cakes and candies, but it was proving difficult. Unlike my partner, I had to work real hard to keep off the pounds. Last month, on my twenty-eighth birthday, I had decided to do something about my weight. Even my six-two frame couldn't disguise my girth. By the time I reached my mid-thirties, I would be the size of a ballast balloon if I didn't do something about it.

Walking out into the blistering sun, I glanced across at my parked black-and-white cruiser and froze. Max was kneeling by the vehicle's open door, his department-issue Sig Sauer P266 drawn, staring at a drugged-out skank in her early twenties. She held a fistful of cash in one hand and a Ruger in the other, pointing the weapon directly at him.

Seeing me, Max shouted a warning. Then everything seemed to happen in slow motion. I let the tray fall to the ground while the woman fired twice at Max. The first bullet missed, but the second was a direct hit, tearing flesh and shattering bones as it burrowed into him. Then she spun around to shoot me as I reached for my weapon.

I woke with a start. I was sweating and breathing rapidly. The dream was always the same, but now I seemed to be having it more frequently. Now it was once or twice a month. I had no idea why. It wasn't as if I was any more stressed than usual.

I sat up in my creaky single bed. Across the dingy room, my old friend Max Creeling slept peacefully in the second bed, his wheelchair close by. Even though the shooting had paralyzed Max from the waist down, he didn't seem to be tortured by the same demons as me.

I checked the alarm clock on my bedside table. It was just one minute past six. Time to rise and shine. I had only celebrated my thirty-third birthday, but no trace was left of that young, fresh-faced cop of just a few years ago. Although now slim and muscular, I had aged noticeably, my hair had thinned, and crow's feet extended around my eyes.

I reluctantly pushed myself up and rolled out of bed. Trying to motivate myself was a real struggle. Still, I was lucky. A massive increase in pollution had left many of us 'oldies,' all of us over thirty, struggling to breathe and unable to walk very far. At least I had my health and my strength.

Slipping on my black t-shirt and sweatpants, I trudged to the window and twisted the grubby wand to open the dirty plastic blinds. I peered out. The sun was just coming up over the city and, even viewed through the dust-smeared glass, it was a beautiful vista. If I pulled up the blinds, opened the window, leaned out, and twisted my head I could just glimpse the ocean.

Before I came to view the studio apartment, the agent had bragged about its ocean views. He forgot to mention that you needed to be a contortionist to see them, but I didn't mind. The small space had the one thing I needed most: it was cheap. And before Max had arrived, the apartment seemed plenty big to me. But now with both my friend and I living there, it had become claustrophobic.

I had to take Max in. We were comrades in arms, and if it hadn't been for the shooting outside the donut store and my slow reaction, Max wouldn't have lost the use of his legs. He was given a disability award and got pensioned off the force. After the shooting, I had suffered panic attacks, so I handed in my badge right after Max retired. In retrospect, it was probably the stupidest thing I'd ever done, but I'd always followed my impulses. Even when they turned out to be wrong.

Max had been in a desperate state when he'd arrived at my place six months ago. He had little money left, despite the chunk of change he'd collected when he'd given up work. Now he only had his small pension left to live on. Max had fallen behind on the rent at his place, and the landlord had thrown him out with barely a day's notice. At the time, I didn't ask what had happened but later discovered that my old friend had a major gambling problem—one he swore he had under control now.

I twisted the wand to flick the blinds shut and walked across to the tiny bathroom. I had just a few minutes to wash and shave before I left. I had no savings left, so if I didn't work I wouldn't be able to eat and risked both of us getting thrown out on the street. My landlord wouldn't take any more sob stories. He had plenty of others willing to rent the room.

I turned on the faucet, pushed my plastic razor under the trickle of liquid, and managed to pull the blunt blade over my stubble a couple of times before the water cut off. It was only Thursday, but we must have used up this week's quota already.

Putting down the razor, I glanced across at the clock. Time to go.

3

I ran the two miles in record time but still only got to the *Los Angeles Free Times* loading bay just before six-thirty where already more than eighty people were waiting. I pushed up against the high brick wall at the perimeter and scanned the competition. Only a few people were older than me. Most were in their teens or early twenties. No one talked. I had seen most of them before. Some, like me, had been coming here for months. Others turned up for a few weeks and then, for one reason or another, couldn't hack it anymore and disappeared.

The boss, Joe Parson, a big, burly man in his mid-twenties wearing shorts and a ratty t-shirt, came out of the adjacent office building and walked across to climb onto the loading dock. All eyes followed his every move.

"Okay, you know the drill. If you're chosen, jump up and let me smell your breath," Parson said. "So let's start. Who wants South West Eight?"

Pandemonium broke out as people raised their hands and shouted. I moved forward too, my hand up. Parson smiled. He was well aware of the power he wielded. He waited until the shouting subsided before pointing to a young, fit-looking woman. "You," he said.

The woman eagerly stepped onto the dock and opened her mouth to breathe into Parson's face. The big man nodded and handed her a slip of paper. She got the job, and the crowd waited expectantly for more work to be given out as she headed into the building.

The Pennsylvanian route was next up, and a red-faced man was chosen from the crowd. This time, though, when he breathed into Parson's face, he was dismissed. "Stay off the barley," Parson said as the man slunk away.

The shouting started up again. I waved my hands, desperate to get the big man's attention. It worked. Parson pointed at me. Envious eyes watched as I pushed through the crowd to join him on the loading dock. Like the others, I was expected to breathe into Parson's face, but unlike the previous guy, I passed the sniff test.

Parson handed me a slip of paper with a single word written on it: *Pennsylvania.* Getting the Pennsylvanian route was a coup. It was one of the larger delivery areas, and landing the job meant I would earn enough money to put food on the table today. Many of the remaining crowd would not be so lucky. I knew how that felt. I went to the dock every morning and was fortunate if I was chosen twice a week.

The so-called experts loved to say the economy was getting better, but the fact was that only a few led such blessed lives. They were part of the twenty percent, the *one-fifths* as they were known, who had regular work and incomes.

The economy had collapsed twenty years ago, at around the same time climate change was really starting to kick in. The world had never recovered. Now official statistics showed unemployment at about ten percent. Most believed the real figure was closer to eighty.

For a time, I had been a 'one-fifth.' I'd earned a regular wage as a cop and had never worried about unemployment. I had agreed with those who claimed anyone who didn't have a job was just too lazy to look for employment. Since my resignation from the force, I had come to realize just how naive I'd been.

"Paper?" The demand came from a bare-chested man wearing blue cloth shorts. This was Lever. I handed the slip over. Lever glanced at the note and produced his cellphone. He photographed the piece of paper, recording the start time, and then walked down a long line of backpacks. He stopped by one that had the word *Pennsylvania* written on a sticker stuck to its front.

Lever picked the pack up and flung it at me. Catching it, I almost fell backwards.

Lever grinned. "Too much weight?" he asked.

I smiled. "No. It's fine." I ripped the sticker off and swung the bag onto my back. The pack was heavy, but it was important not to show any weakness. Lever would love nothing better than to lose this job for me.

Heading for the entrance, I turned the sticker around and stared at the map on the back. A line of red ink ran from the dock to the start point of newspaper route on Pennsylvania Avenue and then continued to form a large rectangle. This was my delivery route. It was thirty miles—and I had to complete it in eight hours.

Even though it was still early, the sun had already risen high in the sky and the temperature was starting to climb. Soon, it would be like working in a furnace. Not so long ago, climate change had been treated by the then-president as a hoax. He pulled out of global climate treaties and refused to continue any scientific research aimed at trying to solve the problem. The results were catastrophic. The average temperature continued to soar year-in, year-out, and global sea levels had risen rapidly. Cities like Miami disappeared underwater, and, because of the heat, the Midwest became virtually uninhabitable. With the temperature spiking, agricultural output had collapsed too, leaving millions starving.

By the time I got to the start of the route, I was sweating profusely, but I had to keep moving. I was already late. Increasing my pace, I reached into my backpack, pulled out a newspaper and threw it onto the front porch of the first house. As I ran, I repeated the maneuver again and again. Every home had to receive a newspaper whether they wanted it or not. Papers like the *Free Times* had only survived by guaranteeing the few advertisers huge numbers of readers. In some ways it was surprising that newspapers were still being produced. But they had benefited from the massive increase in Internet fees. Using the web was now reserved only for the very wealthy. Few could afford televisions or radios anymore, either, so the free papers were the only way to find out what was happening in the world for most of us. Even so, they operated on a knife-edge.

To cut costs, the papers paid a pittance to the men and women who delivered them: people like me. But it was no use complaining. Someone would always be more than willing to take the job if you didn't want it. To make further economies, there had even been talk of the newspapers using Robos to do the delivery work, but customers had balked so far. For some, the only person they saw all day was the man or woman who delivered the paper.

The small, rundown homes on the Pennsylvania route were a mix of low-cost rentals and cheap owner-occupied houses. Crime and drug culture, though high here, was not as endemic as in some divisions. The cops rarely came into these areas anymore; policing these zones fell to the neighborhood watch. Police were far too busy protecting the rich, who were always complaining about security. These wealthy zones, places like the Brents or the Palaces, were totally enclosed, protected by high walls and electrified fences. They would never allow newspaper delivery workers like me in.

The rich rarely came out of their enclaves, preferring to work in offices within them and send their children to local private schools. The only non-white, non-Christians allowed in were maids, gardeners, and handymen. These were strictly screened over a six-month period before they were given permits to enter. Even then, sometimes it would take at least two hours every morning to get through the checkpoints at the gate. And only stores and shops within the zone were allowed to make deliveries.

As I ran, I glanced up at the sun. It still amazed me how quickly the heat became intolerable. When I had started working for the *Free Times*, I had wondered why deliverers hadn't simply dumped all the papers at the start of the day when it was cooler, and then returned later to get paid. I had never seriously thought to do this and soon learned honesty was a smart move. Those who tried to cheat—and there were a few—were inevitably caught by the inspectors who spot-checked the routes. The newspaper always prosecuted, and cheaters got jailed for up to five years. When they came out of prison, they never worked again and would spend the rest of their lives homeless and begging on the streets.

The delivery job, though straightforward, had its dangers. I knew there were places on every route where you had to increase your pace or risk getting robbed—or worse. I had heard of deliverers being mugged at the end of their route by thieves who took their empty backpacks and returned to the dock to collect their pay.

The newspaper did nothing to stop this. The way they saw it, if someone else collected your wage that was your problem. They only cared that the papers were delivered within the allotted hours. Otherwise your earnings were docked and you were told not to return.

As I worked, to relieve my boredom I often scanned the paper for news—not that there was much of that. Generally, newspapers were filled with more or less the same stories every morning—politicians talking about how well everything was going, how unemployment was falling, and wages were rising. There were numerous celebrity updates too, keeping readers abreast of who was marrying who, who was divorcing, who, and who was pregnant, along with major picture stories showing celebrities at work and play, 'living the life.'

Today the headline on the front page read: *NSC defeats Krail rebels in the east.* For once, this was real news. The Krails lived in the wastelands and hills outside the city. They robbed and murdered anyone stupid enough to venture out and made raids into the metropolis from time to time to carry out home invasions and terrorize the local populace.

I hated the Krails and was always thankful for the work of the National Security Council. In a world that was dying on its feet, this organization and its officers were the only people who protected society from criminals like the Krails.

CHAPTER TWO

A FTER I FINISHED THE ROUTE and collected my pay, I always went to the same place: the Pueson Hills Tip. It's where I was now, scouring the mountain of garbage, my mask on, trying to shut out the putrid smell and gas that drifted across the towering mounds of fly-infested waste.

I couldn't afford *not* to go to the rubbish tip. Like the thousands who lived on 'The Hills,' without the garbage, I wouldn't survive. Most times I would find something of use, maybe a can of food or a piece of clothing. It always astonished me how much some people threw away. I guess most of it came from the rich zones. No one else could afford to dump anything so valuable.

The Hills was just one of ten massive 'tips' dotted around Los Angeles. Years ago, few bothered to go near these pollution time bombs. But now, each one had its own community of permanent residents. Known simply as Pickers, many lived in huts made of garbage while others slept out on the carpet of rubbish.

As the number of Pickers had risen, so had the competition. There were stories of people getting knifed for a tin of beans or beaten to a pulp for a carton of rancid milk. There had even been murders as the Pickers fought amongst themselves for the best offerings.

The arrival of the trucks usually brought the violence to a head. It used to be that the large, eight-wheeled garbage wagons would come in at all times of the day, but now a strict timetable had been set up. The trucks only entered The Hills in the afternoon and were always protected by armed guards.

I timed my visit to coincide with the trucks' arrival. The trick was to wait close to the dumping point. Today I watched as the line of trucks weaved along the ridge of The Hills, avoiding the small fires constantly smoking and burning amongst the waste.

I always tried to calculate exactly where the vehicle column would come to a halt. This was important, not just to give me the greatest chance of finding the best garbage, but also to prevent the huge vehicles from tipping garbage on me. Pickers died this way all the time, crushed under mountains of waste.

As the trucks arrived, lining up to discharge their loads, everyone cautiously moved forward. I adjusted my breathing mask and moved forward, too. Noxious materials were always amongst the new waste, and I was grateful for even the scant protection my mask provided.

The hinged backs of the dumper trucks rose in unison releasing their filthy cargo, allowing it to thunder onto the ground. The crowd moved forward eagerly scanning the garbage. This was the moment of greatest excitement and greatest danger.

As the vehicles drove off, I spotted a can of tomatoes and reached down for it, only to have the tin snatched up by a skinny youth. He stared at me, daring me to try and take it, but that would have been stupid. I knew he was probably carrying a switchblade and willing to use it. I ignored the kid and moved forward. I saw another can and this time managed to grab it. The black and dented tin's label boasted that Mario's Dark Kidney Beans were "rich, plump, and tender—guaranteed to make any salad a meal." I quickly dropped the bean can into one of my pant pockets, just as a small child walked by. I watched him as he dived into the muck to grab a plastic car. Grasping the toy, the boy suddenly screamed out as he started to slide down the hill of garbage. Instinctively, I reached out and held the kid by his arm. Holding the little boy tight, I pulled him to safety.

"Thanks," an adult voice said. I turned to see a man in his thirties wearing a mask, a bowler hat, and jeans. He held out his hand to me and I shook it. "Come on, Brin," the man said to the child who, smiling now and still holding the toy vehicle, shuffled away.

Pulling his mask down, the child turned. "Thank you!" he shouted back at me.

Over the next few hours, I managed to find a couple more undamaged tins of food—a can of asparagus and some mushroom soup—before I called it a day. It was a good haul, and I was feeling happy as I half-walked, half-slid back down the hill. Reaching the bottom, I headed out of the tip, stopping for a moment to catch a piece of card blowing in the wind. Wiping away coffee grounds, I stared at it. It was an old postcard of Santa Monica Pier.

A great find. I would keep the card to add to my collection.

I was feeling good as I walked up the rickety tenement stairs. It had been a great day. I'd gotten work, my trip to The Hills had been a success, and I'd been able to afford the small bag of groceries I was carrying up to the apartment. But that was before I opened my apartment door.

Three guys stood around Max and his wheelchair. They filled the room. The two biggest men stood either side of my friend, gripping his arms. They faced a small, weasel-faced guy who clutched a Louisville Slugger.

I knew them. They were part of a local gang, and I had a pretty good idea why they were here. Gambling was enormously popular nowadays. People who had almost reached rock bottom decided to literally take one final roll of the dice. They reasoned that, no matter how badly life knocked them around, their luck had to come good just once. Pawning anything they had, they would journey out to one of the numerous casinos that had sprouted up all over the city. Inevitably, they would lose and loan sharks would squeeze them for what little they had left. McGuire, the man holding the bat, was one of them.

I slowly put the grocery bags down on the floor. "Max, you didn't tell me we were going to have company," I said, stalling. "We don't have enough food to go around."

"Don't worry, we just came by to collect our pound of flesh," McGuire said.

So Max *had* started gambling again. "How much?" I asked.

"Ten large."

"It was a sure thing," Max said.

I shook my head. Unlike some, Max had started betting when he really did have money and still lost it all. Now, apparently, he'd gone back—with the same result.

"Your boy Max here has been dodging us for days. But it's time to square the books," McGuire said. He hit his open hand with the baseball bat. "Normally the payment is five grand per leg, but since Max here ain't got his, we figure five an arm ought to do instead."

I stared at the men. Max had put me in an impossible position. No way was I going to come out of this ahead. I took a deep breath, readying myself. These were big men and used to violence, but they probably weren't trained like I was.

I hoped not, anyway.

Moving forward, I pulled the baseball bat from McGuire's hands and brought it hard down on the biggest man's arms. He fell to the floor, writhing in pain. His partner moved across to deal with me, but I had anticipated that. I swung the bat around and brought it smashing down on his legs. Screaming in pain, the man fell, joining his companion on the floor. I handed the bat back to McGuire.

"That was stupid," he remarked. "Next time, I'll come back with more than just a baseball bat and two men." Signaling them to get up and out, McGuire and his men headed for the door.

"How did they find you?" I asked Max as we packed.

"They must have spotted me when I was having lunch."

I nodded. That made sense. Max was a creature of habit and always ate at the same spot, at the bright blue NSC catering truck parked downtown. It wouldn't take long for anyone who was seriously looking for him to work that out. Since gambling away his lump sum disability award and being unable to get work, Max had had to rely on his small pension and charity to survive. He was not alone. Hundreds lined up along Crenshaw Street for the free truck handout. Without this, lots of people would starve.

Some people were too proud to wait for the free food, afraid that someone might see them. Max had felt the same at first, reasoning that the truck was maybe not so much for him but for the really needy. Though prepared to accept my offer of free accommodation, he couldn't and *wouldn't* take my food. So before long, he overcame his reservations and lined up with the rest for the lunchtime giveaway.

But Max didn't just come to the lunch for food. I knew that he enjoyed hanging out on Crenshaw with the NSC officers. Like me, he really admired the organization. The men reminded us of our former colleagues on the force. If Max was able-bodied, he would have done what I had done and applied for a post with them. But getting a position as an NSC officer was hugely competitive—so if you were disabled, you had no chance at all.

The NSC used the lunch to promote its work. A large colorful sign hung on the side of the catering trunk with the words "NSC – Forging the Future for You" written in silver lettering beside a picture of a family with their backs to a bright sunrise.

The lunchtime hot soup and sandwiches on offer were given out by a bevy of tall, good-looking men and women—NSC officers all. They understood that the people who came needed companionship as well as food, someone to talk to and remind them they were not invisible. Max had told me he knew that feeling of invisibility well. If you're disabled, to many people, you might as well not be there at all.

Once and only once, Max had talked to me candidly about the loss of his legs. I had told him about my recurring dream, and he had admitted that he had gone to sleep every night after the incident wishing that when he woke up his legs would miraculously work again. Back then it was the reason that he had made light of his "rehabilitation." He'd believed he didn't really need a wheelchair because he would be walking again soon. In fact, after the shooting, instead of worrying about losing the use of his legs, Max confided he was more concerned about me. He knew I felt responsible for what had happened, believing I could have prevented it. Sometimes, Max said, he felt that I would have preferred if I'd been crippled instead.

It was a pretty astute observation.

"So you spotted their car while you were having lunch?" I asked.

Max nodded. In downtown L.A., you don't see many vehicles anymore, so he said that this one stood out, even though it had parked way down the road.

"But I still didn't put two and two together," Max said as he pushed the last of his clothes into his bag. "I was too busy trying to fix my wheelchair. It wouldn't move. Something had locked. One of those tall, blonde NSC officers came up to help, so I forgot about the car."

Max looked over at me. "Do we really need to leave?"

"Yeah, we do." McGuire would keep his word. He had to. He had lost face. I had met the man before, just after Max arrived. He still owed the loan shark money even though he'd stopped gambling. I used all my savings up to pay off McGuire and had nothing left. So neither of us had any way now of paying the loan shark back. If we didn't get out, we would both end up dead.

"When did you start betting again."

"A few weeks ago."

It was a surly response, something I'd come to expect. I knew Max hated being dependent on me. And now he had chalked up one more reason to feel indebted. I picked up both our bags and looked around the apartment. Four dirty, whitewashed brick walls, a couple of single beds, two bedside tables, a wardrobe that leaned to one side, and a small kitchen table with three chairs. This had been my life for the best part of a year. It wasn't much but, strangely, I would miss the place.

It was home.

"I really don't want to go," Max said again.

"What?"

"You heard me."

I shook my head. "We need somewhere to hide out. McGuire is going to come back with reinforcements. I was lucky but there's no way I'm going to win next time."

I stared at Max, who said nothing. "Look, I still have a few friends in Seattle."

"I hate Seattle."

"You've never been! And are you seriously saying that you'd rather stay here and get us both beaten to a pulp?"

Max sighed deeply.

"Well, are you?"

There was a long silence. Then: "No…I'm sorry."

"So, Seattle's okay?" I asked, determined to wrestle an admission out of him.

Max nodded. "I guess."

"And you have to swear to me. No more gambling."

Max crossed his heart. "I swear."

A floorboard creaked in the corridor outside. I raised my hand to Max. Something or someone was outside. Surely it couldn't be McGuire back with reinforcements so soon? I yanked the door open, dragging a man inside. I pushed him hard against the wall and pulled back my fist.

"Stop, Hogan!" Max shouted. "He's NSC."

I hesitated and stared at the man. Max was right. He was wearing the traditional blue and white NSC uniform and was not happy. *Shit.* I had almost assaulted an officer. I backed away.

"Sir," I said, "I'm sorry."

"You Hogan Duran?" he growled.

I nodded.

"ID."

I produced my driver's license. The face of a younger, happier, fatter man stared back out from a photo on the document. I hadn't had a car for years but needed to keep the license for identification.

The officer stared at the picture and looked back up at me.

"Changed a bit since then," I said.

He nodded. "I guess that could be you," he said as he handed the document back. Then he pulled an official-looking brown envelope from his pocket and handed it to me.

"Don't do that again, sir, or next time I'll be forced to arrest you," the officer said as he pulled open the door.

When he'd gone, I stared at the envelope. Max moved to my side. We both knew what it was. I had applied to be an NSC officer three times. Twice before I'd gotten an envelope back just like this. And twice my hopes had been dashed when I'd opened it. Maybe it was third time lucky...or maybe not.

"You going to open it or just look at it?"

"Max, please," I said. He knew just how much this meant to me. I was allowed to take my time. Taking a deep breath, I ripped the envelope open and pulled out an official- looking letter. I scanned the note quickly as Max peered over my shoulder.

"Well?"

CHAPTER THREE

THE STATION: A SEETHING MASS of humanity. Some came with hope in their hearts, ready to embark on the journey of a lifetime. For others, it was the only place they had left to go. They had reached rock bottom. Day or night, the scene was always the same: Transporters arrived and departed constantly, full of people desperate to get away from here, from there, from everywhere. Others wandered around the Station aimlessly. These were the homeless, the addicts, the criminals, the thieves, and deadbeats. They spent their time begging or looking for something to steal.

And there was always tension in the air. A fight could break out at any moment as these tired and hungry people reached their wits' ends and lashed out at the world.

Max and I had been waiting there two hours, which was at least one hour and fifty-nine minutes too long but neither of us minded. I kept reaching into my pocket to pull out the letter and stare at it.

"You'll wear it out, buddy," said a smiling Max after I had brought the note out a tenth time. "Just accept it. Next stop: Easy Street."

I pushed the letter back into my pocket. I still couldn't believe it. I'd been accepted. That was the good news. The bad news was I knew that this letter only confirmed that I had been chosen for NSC *training*. It was incredibly difficult to get this far, but even so, only a very few would make it to through to the next stage—to become officers. Frankly, I had grave doubts I could make it that far.

Max tapped me on my shoulder and pointed to a transporter that had just pulled in to Dock 10. It had the word Seattle printed above its windshield. It was Max's ride. "Okay, Hogan, looks like it's my time to go."

I moved behind Max's wheelchair and pushed it through the seething crowd towards the vehicle. It was, like all public transporters nowadays, driverless. So since there was no one to help, it was up to me to put Max's ticket into the scanner and to lower him into in his allotted seat. After that, I folded his wheelchair and carried the chair to the luggage rack at the front.

As I finished storing the chair, I spotted an attractive woman in her mid-thirties walk up to Max. I watched as she checked the seat number on her ticket. "That is twenty-two N isn't it?" I heard the woman say to Max as she pointed to the vacant seat next to him.

Max smiled. "It sure is. And you have the luck to be sitting next to Max Creeling." He held out his hand. "Great to meet you."

The woman smiled and sat next to him as I returned.

"Okay, Max, time to go. See if you can get someone to help you with the chair at the other end."

"I think I can organize that," the woman said. "I'm Lisa." She pushed out her hand and I shook it.

"Pleased to meet you, Lisa. Thank you for your kind offer. Now, Max, don't forget when you get to Seattle to keep out of trouble."

"Will do."

I high-fived Max. "Bye. And behave yourself."

"Always."

I turned quickly and headed for the transporter's exit door. Almost as soon as I had stepped down from the vehicle, the door slid shut, the last passenger just managing to squeeze on. As the transporter drove off, Max peered out of the window and winked at me before turning to speak animatedly with Lisa. It looked like he had struck it lucky.

I missed him already.

My transporter would be in next. Dock 20. I started to walk towards the number 20 sign, scanning the crowd for those who were waiting for the NSC Transit transporter like me.

A tall, handsome man in his early twenties stepped in front of me, momentarily blocking my way. I glanced across at him. I knew the type. Dangerous and arrogant but the sort of asshole that women love. In fact, two young beautiful girls were with him: long legs, flowing blonde hair, angelic faces. They were obviously twins.

A commotion came from behind, and a middle-aged, scruffy, worn-down man pushed through the crowd, a rusty shotgun in hand. "Hey, you!" he screamed at the guy with the girls. "Those are my *daughters*, you son of a bitch."

The handsome man turned, taking in the man and his gun.

"Really," he replied. "Then I guess I owe you for raising such lovely pleasure units."

"They aren't pleasure units, they're my *girls*, and they're only seventeen."

"Oh, God…I didn't know," the handsome man said, looking shocked. "They swore they were fifteen." He grabbed one of the teenagers and starting to kiss her passionately.

"You bastard," the older man said, and raised the shotgun, ready to fire. The handsome man pushed away the girl he was kissing, spun around, and yanked the weapon from the father's hands in one motion. In an instant, the father was looking down the barrel of his own gun.

"The only reason I don't shoot you right now is 'cause I'm afraid this rusty piece of shit might blow up in my face." The younger man cracked the gun open and dumped the shells onto the floor. Then he pulled a gleaming handgun from his trousers and leveled it directly at the father's head. "This, on the other hand, is in perfect working order. Care to test it?"

The father lunged forward, but I grabbed him, pulling him back. "That's enough."

The handsome man stared at me. "Well, thank you," he said, stuffing his pistol back into his pants. "You should thank him too, Dad," he said to the girls' father, "you could have got yourself hurt." He turned away to look at the girls. "Ladies—it's been a pleasure. I'm sure you won't forget your time with Jake Teerman."

"Bye, Jake," one of them shouted as she consoled her teary-eyed sister.

The man, Jake, quickly headed towards the transporter that had just pulled up at Dock 20.

"I guess some girls like that kind of thing," a voice behind me said.

I turned. The woman who'd just spoken was strikingly attractive, with long dark hair, piercing blue eyes, and a button nose. She was dressed in form-fitting jeans and a blue blouse that hugged her shapely body. She carried an antique leather holdall.

She held out her hand. "Ruby Mason."

"Hogan Duran. Pleased to meet you" I said, shaking her hand and pointing at the NSC Transporter. "You getting on board?"

Ruby smiled proudly. "Yep. And you?"

I nodded and glanced at Jake Teerman, who was climbing up the transporter's stairs.

"He's going as well. I thought the NSC was more selective."

"I guess not," Ruby said.

About a hundred of us were cramped on board. Most were in their late teens and early twenties, mainly young men but with a sprinkling of women. I knew I was an old man by their standards. It was a pretty big handicap, and since Max's shooting, my confidence had never really returned. Was I up to this?

The transporter had been pretty quiet from the start, with only a few talking to one another. That was the sensible thing to do. We didn't know exactly what our training would involve, and to give too much away about yourself at this stage was not a smart strategy.

Ruby and I hadn't spoken much, either. I'd told her about me being an ex-cop. She'd told me that she was a waitress who had just been fired from her job. The news of NSC acceptance had been the lifeline she'd needed. To keep the conversation going but avoiding any more personal talk, I pointed at the transporter driver. "Haven't seen one of those for years."

"Me neither," Ruby said.

It was a surprise to both of us. Nowadays, cars and trucks were almost all driverless. When they were first introduced, people had willingly given up their vehicles and relied on driverless taxis to get around. Before long, all trucks had been made driverless, too, and as demand for 'driven' cars fell, the industry collapsed: factories closed and workers were made redundant, joining the thousands of professional drivers in the ranks of the unemployed.

The NSC was one of the few employers who kept their drivers on, not trusting the security of driverless vehicles. Onboard computers could be hacked, they reasoned. It was difficult to accomplish, of course, but it was a risk the organization wasn't prepared to take.

The view from the vehicle was a revelation to me, too, even though as a cop, I had traveled all over the city. In the four years since resigning from the force, the landscape had changed dramatically. I could see the wealthy zones with their well-lit stores, malls, and schools. These were surrounded by rows of affluent suburban homes, some of which had glistening swimming pools in their back yards. Cars shunted along the wide, clean boulevards, and children played happily in the lush green parks. The zones were protected by high steel-mesh fences hung with huge searchlights. Gun-toting guards, walking with vicious-looking dogs on leashes, manned checkpoints along the border.

In contrast, most of the city's other zones looked like they'd been bombed out. There were no green spaces: the schools were huge, gray, factory-like buildings; the few stores were tiny, temporary structures; and hardly any cars traveled the crumbling roads that often looked impassable anyway. Homes were, for the most part, a mixture of temporary-looking Nissan huts or constructions built out of old wood and corrugated metal sheets.

As the transporter sped on and darkness fell, the signs of decay and dereliction increased. Tents replaced houses and roads became fewer and fewer. When the vehicle finally left what remained of the town and descended from the freeway down onto the open road, the lights inside were dimmed. People slumped back in their chairs, trying to get as comfortable as possible to sleep.

"Night," said Ruby, shutting her eyes.

"Night," I said, and did the same.

I awoke hours later, my legs aching, my back in pain. I really was getting old.

I stared out and saw that the sun had just started to peek over the horizon. Soon it would be high in the sky, streaming through the transporter's tinted windows. If I was to die and somehow found myself in purgatory, it would probably look like this: dirty brown wasteland stretching out as far as the eye could see. On the horizon was a mountain range. But these boasted no romantic, snow-covered summits glistening in the sun: just steep, hostile, rocky escarpments layered with brown dust.

Ruby opened her eyes. "Hi," she said, stretching and pulling herself up.

"Morning."

Ruby turned to look out the window. She shivered. "Is this Hell?" she asked.

"Sure looks like it."

"Three more hours," Ruby said, yawning.

"Yeah, maybe," I said, peering at the small clock positioned high over the driver's head. I reached into my pocket for my old flip phone, and then remembered we'd had to leave all electronic gear with the driver. The NSC expressly forbade anyone to carry anything that could be used to reveal where we were going. I doubted if the clock really showed the correct time. It would be too easy to work out where you were from the time traveled.

Ruby gave a start. "Oh my God." She was staring out the window. I followed her gaze. In the distance, a band of bikers were riding through the wasteland, heading towards the transporter. I recognized them. "Krails," I said. "I've never seen them up close."

Others on the transporter had seen the Krails, too. They watched fascinated as the gang approached. As they came closer, I could make out the lined, tough faces of the riders. Although all were dressed in the same tight black leathers, some wore black bandanas or had long scarves covering their necks and faces. Many had grown their hair out, letting it fall down to their waist, while others had it shaved off completely. It was hard to tell the women from the men. All looked equally tough, with lined faces browned in the sun.

More than anything else, Krails were proud of their bikes. Despite the dust, each machine had been meticulously cleaned so their chrome and steel handle bars shone. Some riders had bows slung over their shoulders, quivers of arrows hanging from their belts. Others carried long hunting knives stuck into ornate belts, and handguns stuffed into leather holsters. The man on the lead bike looked huge and terrifying. He was bald, and his face was crisscrossed with long scars.

Ruby made a face. "Disgusting. How can anyone live like that?"

"Maybe they ask the same thing about us," I said as the transporter accelerated away.

Staring back, I saw the big bald man, the Krail leader, raise his hand and indicate the rocky outcrops on the horizon. Pulling his bike around, he started to ride in the direction he'd indicated. The others followed in V-formation.

The transporter sped over the flat wasteland towards a vast steel-domed fortress that peaked over high metal walls. Two massive iron doors lay directly ahead of our vehicle. Towers with reinforced bulletproof glass domes loomed on each side of the gates. I could see NSC guards moving around inside. They stared at our transporter and, as it came to a halt outside the compound, opened the doors to allow it to enter. The transporter drove through and stopped in front of the fortress. Behind us, the gates swung closed.

Our vehicle parked in front of what was obviously the main building. This was constructed out of reinforced glass and silver steel. Now that we were inside, I could see that the fortress formed the shape of a letter H, its walls running to the left and right and parallel to either side of the steel frontage into which a huge NSC logo had been embedded.

Two lone towers rose either side of the domed fort. One had a base of shining steel that was some one hundred and fifty feet high and topped by a round glass structure. The other tower, on the opposite side and some distance from the fortress, was smaller and completely windowless. To the right of the fortress stood a smaller concrete building that I later found out was the canteen.

Ruby and I peered out at the brigade of uniformed NSC officers, their weapons out, who had moved to surround our vehicle.

"Impressive, huh?" I said.

"You could say that," Ruby said, her eyes wide.

The transporter driver, a stocky man with a cropped military haircut, stood up. He waved his hands to quiet the chatter that had risen as our vehicle pulled into the compound.

"Everyone off. Single file," he ordered.

Standing and grasping our overnight bags, Ruby and I joined the line filing out of the vehicle. As we left, two NSC officers carrying tablets checked our ID and names against the listings they had.

"Duran, Hogan, you are now Candidate number four-five-four-five-nine. Don't forget it," the officer said after matching up my name.

From the vehicle, the driver also watched each and every one of us with eagle-eyes. Glancing back, I saw he had stopped Jake and taken his gun off him.

A tall, movie-star handsome officer waited in the center of the square and introduced himself as Commander Beecham. He urged the new arrivals to move quickly. Anyone who was deemed to be too slow got a jolt from electric prods carried by the NSC officers. Ruby and I were directed into one of the ten rows. Jake walked into the line behind us.

Commander Beecham shouted, "Attention!" He stepped back to allow a hovering glider ball to fly past. This circular steel orb was the size of a basketball. It had a tinted screen on its front and out of this stared the lined face of a man who looked incredibly old, and was maybe in his mid-fifties, with a jarhead, buzz cut and wearing the NSC Superior officer Uniform, of blue, white, and red. Five stars were visible on the man's epaulets: a general.

Technology had obviously moved on a pace over the past few years. I had never seen a glider ball in my life. It was an impressive piece of kit.

The glider ball hovered through the rows of new arrivals as, from it, the man spoke: "Welcome, candidates. My name is General Stoker. You have just arrived at National Security Council Base Camp Seventeen, or as most come to know it…*Hell on Earth.*"

The glider ball halted directly in front of me. General Stoker eyeballed me for a few moments before moving away.

"You have all agreed to be tested on every conceivable level of mental, emotional, and physical hardship," General Stoker said. "Our job here is to make you wish you'd never been born. We will subject you to every form of cruelty, depravity, and humiliation you can imagine. You will be scarred, starved, and forced to wonder why God played the cruel trick of ever putting you on this miserable earth. You will ask yourself a simple question… 'Is *anything* worth this?' My answer is just as simple. YES. IT. IS."

The glider ball hovered by me again as I waited for the general to say more.

"If you have what it takes to be a member of the NSC, rest assured you will be one of the top wage-earners in the country. You and your families will live in the finest houses built just for NSC members. You will eat the tastiest foods, enjoy the greatest entertainment, and live better than you could ever have thought imaginable. In short," he said, "you will live like gods."

I saw a heavily tattooed hulk of a man in a tee and jeans lean across to his neighbor. "Does being a god come with full medical?" he stage-whispered.

The glider ball moved rapidly along the line to eye the whisperer. "What was that?" General Stoker asked.

The tattooed man hesitated. "Nothing, sir," he said.

General Stoker softened. "Just a bit of levity, then?" he asked the new arrival. "Yes, sir."

A list of names scrolled up the ball's screen. One name was bolded. "You're Phillips? Marcus Phillips?" the general asked.

The tattooed man nodded and clicked his heels together. "Yes, sir."

The glider ball spun away at speed to stop in front of Commander Beecham. "Beecham, Candidate Phillips is dismissed."

Back in line, Phillips started to tear up as Beecham nodded to two NSC officers. They walked to Phillips, pulled him out of line, and frog-marched him back to the transporter.

General Stoker's voice boomed out from the glider ball again. "I know you are all thinking that I'm being harsh, but believe me, I am doing him a favor. That quick wit of his assures me he's not the one we are looking for."

There was a low murmur from our ranks. Had the general really said 'the one?' Was he implying that only *one* of us would be chosen?

"Yes, you heard right," General Stoker continued, seemingly reading our minds. "Just one. You're all the best. But we want to narrow it down to the best of the best. The one that can rise to the top... Now, take a look at the person next to you."

I locked eyes with Ruby. Behind us, Jake turned to stare at a thin-faced African American man.

"That person is not your friend, nor is he or she your teammate. That person wants to take this opportunity away from you. That person is standing between you and your place amongst us and should be treated accordingly. That person is an obstacle to be overcome, like so many others that you will encounter here," General Stoker said.

"And to that one candidate destined to rise above the rest, I look forward to welcoming you into the NSC."

CHAPTER FOUR

A S WE LINED UP TO shower, the group's mood became noticeably more subdued. I had known it was going to be tough to join the NSC, but I never thought the odds were going to be this bad. Of course, most of the others were younger than I, so it was just possible that, if they failed, they would get a second chance. But I knew that wasn't going to happen to me.

"Clothes, Candidate," an NSC officer ordered as I reached the door of the shower room. Undressing quickly, I handed my t-shirt and pants to the officer. He motioned for me to also remove my underwear. "I want *all* your clothes, Candidate."

I slipped off my boxers and handed them over. "You'll be redressed on the other side," the officer said, as he ordered me to enter the shower room, a long white-tiled room with showerheads set in the wall every five feet or so.

All of us took our places under a shower, which immediately pumped out hot, high-pressure water. It was a marvel. I hadn't been washed like this in years. In fact, I couldn't even remember the last time I'd had a shower. Clean tap water just wasn't available in large amounts unless you had money to burn.

The water thundered down on my head. Through the spray, I could see that all were enjoying the experience. Despite the mix of sexes in the room, no one seemed self-conscious either, except for one woman. She had purposely chosen the shower in the corner and had her back turned to the others.

Ruby.

Suddenly the showers cut off. A siren boomed from overhead and an automated computer voice demanded: "Leave now. Leave now."

We marched single file out of the room as another batch of the new arrivals entered.

Exiting the shower room and still wet and naked, we entered a second tiled room. Once again, I noticed Ruby preferred modesty, wrapping her arms around her breasts to cover them.

We were ordered to line up against two steel-topped tables. One was for men, the other for the women. Rows of military-issue boxers were placed on the men's table. The women had the same boxers and gray sports bras to put on.

As I quickly pulled my briefs up, white-coated men and women entered the room from a side door. They split up into two teams of six, one team heading for the men's table, the other to the women's table. The first of the team examined my eyes, a second looked down my throat. Other doctors, each with different specialties, followed to check us over one by one.

The examinations were completed silently and without emotion. By now we had become desensitized to humiliation, so no one objected to the medical inspections. I simply tolerated the prodding and pawing and cavity-searching.

After our batch of candidates had been examined, a silver door at the far end slid open. We were all ordered to exit through it and, as we left, a new group entered behind us, lining up for their medical check.

The next room we were led into was the cerebral scan room, which looked like a hair salon designed by the Devil himself. It was completely white and filled with yet more medical staff. Chairs with large, black, dome-shaped helmets attached were lined up against the far wall. Candidates were already seated in the chairs as I entered. Ordered to wait, I watched as doctors pressed small switches on the backs of each helmet and stared at a series of indicators visible on the headgear. Most candidates looked unaffected by the process, but one started to violently shake and convulse.

A doctor hit the switch to stop the machine, and, pulling the helmet back, allowed the candidate to fall to the floor. Two NSC officers walked across with a gurney and hoisted the man's body onto it.

"Candidate seven-nine-eight-seven-dash-nine. Unfit for duty," a medic announced flatly as the gurney was carried out through a sliding door at the back of the room. I glanced across at Ruby, who smiled back nervously.

I'd had a scan like this when I was a kid and fell off my bike. In those days, you had to lie down on a runner and slide into a claustrophobic metal tunnel. They didn't find anything wrong with me, but the experience was profoundly unsettling and left me with a deep fear of any kind of brain scan. To me it was and always would be as strange and menacing as voodoo medicine.

These particular helmet scanners were obviously far more high-tech than anything I had ever encountered, and I guessed were for discovering psychological defects that would make me unsuitable for becoming an officer. It was a frightening thought; I could be failed simply because this machine found something it didn't like.

I felt a bead of sweat drip down the side of my face and reached up quickly to wipe it away.

"You okay?" Ruby asked, concerned.

"Yeah, sure, no problem," I said.

"Next group!" a doctor shouted.

"That'll be us." Ruby headed for one of the doctors. I followed to take a seat under a black helmet.

I raised my hand before the doctor could pull the helmet down. "What happened to the other guy?"

"Who?"

"The one on the gurney."

"Psycho-emotional problems. Clearly unsuitable."

"So that thing can see that?" I pointed to the helmet above me.

"The cerebral scan searches the brain thoroughly and instantly translates the data into many variables that can contribute to mental illness, including childhood trauma and poverty. It's a truly impressive machine," the doctor said with obvious pride. "There can, however, be side effects as a result of this mental probing, but these are nothing to be concerned about. They disappear the moment the helmet is removed. So, are you ready?"

"Yeah, sure." I said.

"Okay, here we go." The doctor lowered the helmet over my head and turned it on.

At first I felt nothing much, just a slight warming around my skull. But the temperature continued to rise, and I began to sweat. At the same time, I felt like something was wriggling around in my mind, searching through every nook and cranny. I tried to concentrate on the room around me, to wipe my mind clear of anything and everything, but bad thoughts kept bubbling to the surface. I remembered when Max had been shot, how the guilt had driven me into a hole or the time when my life had gone into freefall after National Service, before I found my true vocation as a cop.

Then the names *Jackie and Maria* popped into my head. I knew why. I had lied to both of them, convinced them they loved me and that I loved them until I ran out on them. I could see their faces now, floating before me, that last look of hurt and confusion etched into their features. I always ran, I realized. And when things got bad here, I would run too.

My eyes started losing focus and my teeth began to chatter. *What was this thing doing to me?*

I heard a click, and then everything went quiet as the helmet was lifted off my head. "Stay there," the doctor ordered.

I watched as he walked across the room to Commander Beecham. He whispered something, and they both turned to stare at me. Beecham nodded, and the medic broke away to walk back.

It was obvious. They had discovered the true me, a man not worthy of being considered as an NSC officer. Now would come the bad news.

"You can go," the doctor said.

"What?"

"I said you could go."

"You mean…"

"Look, you passed. Just go."

I stood up and walked away rapidly without another word.

The remaining candidates assembled in the gym. Everyone was quiet. waiting to see what was in store. The door opened, and Commander Beecham entered and walked to the center of the room.

"Okay, Candidates, the next test is all about strength." He pointed to the covered benches spread along the walls. Two-foot-high stands with open clawed grips were positioned on either side each bench. A long metal bar lay between the grips.

"Candidates with numbers beginning between one and five go to the benches on that wall. The others lie down on the benches on the other wall."

I went with the first group that included Ruby and Jake and laid back on one of the benches.

Above, the stands and bar slid forward until they were directly over me. Once we were all in position, we were instructed to raise our arms and grip either side of the metal bar.

I looked up at the bar. It had been several years since I'd spent time lifting, but it was something I had really enjoyed. I started at school, and when I went into National Service and later became a cop, I used to lift regularly, at least three or four times a week. Now, of course, simply surviving took up most of my life, but I still managed to occasionally find a way to sneak into a local gym for a quick workout.

NSC officers moved forward to a small keyboard visible on the narrow steel beam. A weight was typed in. Overhead, a computerized voiced announced the weight. One hundred and seventy-five pounds.

We were then asked to lift the bar above our heads and keep it there for at least five seconds before bringing it back down into the clawed grips.

I made my first lift. A second weight was keyed in. "Two hundred and fifty pounds," the overhead computer voice confirmed.

All around me, candidates strained to lift the bar. I heard the clank of metal and frustrated groans as at least a few of them failed the test. I achieved the weight relatively easily. As I waited, holding the bar above me for the set five seconds to elapse, I felt that familiar elation a good lift can bring.

On the next lift, a new number was entered: three hundred pounds. Again I conquered the weight, though this time it was much more difficult. All around me I saw benches emptying as other candidates dropped out.

I glanced over and saw Jake was standing. I didn't see Ruby, so I assumed she was still lifting. But by the time the weight was increased to three hundred and twenty-five pounds, Ruby, along with four of the remaining five lifters, gave up.

I was the only one left.

Most people who don't lift weights think how strong you are depends entirely on your physical prowess—and that is important, yes. But you need more than that to be a great lifter. The real lifting happens in your head. Body and mind must come together, and you must believe in an inverse law of gravity—that the bar *must* and *will* go up.

Commander Beecham walked across to take over from my NSC observer. He typed three hundred and fifty into the keyboard on my bar as the other candidates moved forward to watch. I breathed deeply and steadied myself. I gripped the weight bar tight and, on the lift instruction, pushed my arms up, straightened them and held it high above my head.

"Five, four, three, two, one," Beecham counted slowly. "Lower."

I bought the bar down quickly and let it rest in the open grips above me.

"One more, Candidate?" Beecham asked.

I wasn't sure. The last weight seemed like it was about my limit. If I tried to lift too heavy a load, I could injure myself. Imagine it: having to leave because I was too proud to admit defeat even when I was winning! The smart move was to call it a day.

"Come on, Duran, you can do it," a voice said. "Duran! Duran! Duran…!"

I moved my head and saw Jake leading the others in a chorus of encouragement.

"They think you can do it, Candidate," Beecham said. "So how about it?"

"Okay," I said quickly.

Beecham nodded. "Brave call. How about three hundred and sixty-five?"

Had I *ever* lifted that sort of weight? I didn't think so. "Should be fine," I said with a confidence I didn't feel.

Jake, Ruby, and the other candidates edged forward as Beecham brought the bar's weight up. I lifted my hands again to grasp the bar. How strong was my will? I'd soon find out.

On the instruction "Lift," I pushed the bar up slowly. Who would have thought that the extra fifteen pounds would make that much difference? I started to sweat as I extended my arms, trying to lock them in position. But they wouldn't go. Instead my body swayed under the strain.

Two NSC officers moved forward, ready to take the weight off me, but I shook my head. Stay back. I was going to do it.

Still straining, I managed to lock my arms. I waited. Could I keep the weight in position? The five-count started. "Five, four…"

"Release!" I shouted, and the officers instantly took the weight off me.

There was a collective gasp from the other candidates.

"Bad luck," Beecham said. "But you did good."

Disappointed, I got up slowly, and as I started to walk out of the room, Jake clapped me on the back. "Great try," he said loudly before leaning in close. "Loser," he whispered so only I could hear and walked on.

CHAPTER FIVE

Lunchtime finally arrived. It had been over twenty-four hours since we had eaten, so we were all ravenous by the time we lined up to enter the canteen. There were far fewer of us than when we arrived. I guessed that we were down to around sixty.

Commander Beecham stood at the canteen door in front of a small metal table piled high with boxes. He told us he had important information for us. We would get half an hour to finish our meal, but during this time we would have to take another test.

A collective groan rose up. We thought we would be left in peace to eat, and now we had something else to do. Beecham raised his hand.

"Quiet," he ordered.

The line quieted instantly. "As you know, an NSC officer doesn't just have to have incredible physical abilities. He or she also must act as a representative and spokesperson for our organization. For that, we need someone who we can trust entirely and who is completely truthful. We are going to sit you at tables in groups of five, and as you eat, I want you to discover information about your fellow candidates."

He opened one of the boxes and produced a wafer-thin computer tablet. "Each of you will be given one of these. On touching it, the sensor will recognize who you are, give you the number of the table you will sit at, and reveal a question you have to ask another candidate at your table. Both the person who asks the question and the individual who the question is for must hold their tablets.

"However," Beecham continued, "if the candidate lies about the information he or she supplies, then that person will be eliminated from training."

That seemed simple enough, and the test certainly proved General Stoker's point that NSC officers lacked for nothing. The tablets were clearly bleeding edge technology and each must have cost thousands of dollars.

Ruby put up her hand. "How will we know if it's a lie?"

"The tablets will know, Candidate. Okay, who wants to eat?"

There were shouts of approval, and as the line moved forward, every candidate collected their tablet before entering the canteen. After I had picked up my pad, I saw that it had lit up. The words DURAN, HOGAN, CANDIDATE 4545-9: TABLE 6 scrolled across the screen.

I walked into the canteen. Two rows of metal tables had been positioned in the center. My tablet produced a schematic of the room, and Table 6 flashed green. Sitting down, I stared at the plastic tray in front of me. It held an apple, a plate of carrots, a pack of beef jerky, a granola bar, and a bottle of water.

"Quite a mix," a voice said. I looked up as Ruby sat down opposite.

"Oh, hi. Yeah, someone in the kitchen's got a sense of humor." I said as two other candidates—a tall, well-built African American who introduced himself as Leonard, and a stocky, short haired woman called Christine—joined us. That made four. We were missing one.

"Oh, no," Ruby muttered as Jake walked toward us. She turned her head, avoiding his gaze, but no such luck.

Jake sat next to her and smiled. "Hey, good looking," he said, ignoring me, and then introduced himself to the others and suggested that we all eat before doing the test. Everyone agreed and wolfed our food down despite the menu's strangeness. It all tasted delicious. I couldn't remember when I'd last *seen* a fresh apple, let alone eaten one. The occasional carrots from the cans I found at the garbage tip tasted nothing like these freshly cooked vegetables. The granola bar was a highlight, and the pure protein in the beef jerky was almost too much for my body to take. I felt high after eating it. Although the meal looked like an alien had chosen it, it certainly hit the spot.

I saw that the others were enjoying the meal as much as I was. Leonard had a big grin on his face as he chewed, Ruby was savoring the granola bar she had left to last, and Christine had fallen back in her chair in a state of bliss. Even Jake had been quiet as he ate.

All of us had put the tablets on the table, and the one next to Ruby suddenly started to vibrate. She wiped her fingers on the top of the table, picked it up, read the screen, and looked over at Leonard.

"Leonard," Ruby said, "this is for you." Ruby waited for Leonard to pick up his tablet, before she asked him his question. "What is the stupidest thing you have ever done in your life?"

Leonard smiled. "There are…" He stopped. "I was going to say there are so many, but that's a lie. The stupidest thing I ever did was trying to break into a wealthy zone by climbing the fence. It was electrified, and I fell thirty feet and almost died." Both Ruby and Leonard's tablets glowed green. "Apparently, that's correct," Ruby said.

My tablet vibrated next and, picking it up, I saw there was a question for Jake. "What do you most want to achieve?" I asked him.

Jake held his tablet tight. "That's easy. I want to be an NSC officer. That's it. That's the only thing I want." Both of our tablets glowed green.

The next question was from Leonard for me: "What was the biggest mistake you ever made?" I hesitated before taking a deep breath. "The biggest mistake I've ever made was when I was on the force and let my partner get shot." It was the first time I'd ever admitted this in public, but I knew I had to tell the truth. My tablet turned green and so did Leonard's.

"Wow," said Jake. "That's some confession!"

Then Christine's tablet flashed on and off. She had a question for Ruby.

"Ruby, what was the one piece of information you would not like the others at the table to know?"

Ruby hesitated, her eyes shifting from my face to Jake's and back to mine. "I worked as a stripper a year or so ago when I ran out of money," she said finally. Christine and Ruby's tablets both glowed green.

Jake started to clap. "Good on you, girl. You do what you've got to do. Now, Christine, the question on my tablet for you is: What was your biggest lie?"

Before she could answer, there was a scream from a table at the far end of the room. One of the candidates there had dropped the tablet he was holding and slumped forward.

Ruby looked across at me. "What happened?" I shrugged. I didn't know.

The room went quiet as two NSC officers carrying a gurney moved quickly over to the unconscious candidate. "Take him," Beecham ordered.

The officers picked the man up and carried him out.

"Okay, everyone. Nothing more to see here," Beecham said. "Complete the test."

"You heard the man," Jake said. "What's your answer, Christine?"

"My biggest lie," Christine began, "was that I once told a guy I was pregnant to get rid of him."

Jake and Christine looked down at their tablets. They both turned red. "Apparently, that was a…." Jake never finished his sentence because Christine, gripping her tablet, started to shake violently before falling face-down on the table.

I jumped up and moved around to help the unconscious girl, but before I reached her I was pulled back.

"Leave her, Candidate. That's our job." Commander Beecham raised his hand. I sat back down as two more NSC officers arrived with a gurney and manhandled the unconscious woman onto it.

"She's not dead, is she?" Ruby asked as she watched Christine being carried off on the stretcher.

Commander Beecham smiled. "Of course not. We're not that ruthless. The shock she got through the tablet knocked her out. She'll be awake in a few minutes, and she'll be ready to leave on the next transporter out—one more candidate who couldn't hack it."

Jake smiled. "And one less competitor for us."

Beecham nodded. "That's the spirit, Candidate."

He picked up Christine's tablet and glanced at it. Leonard looked over to read the tablet too, but Beecham turned it away and walked off.

"Did you see what it said, Leonard?" I asked.

"It just showed the correct answer Christine should have given to the question."

"Which was?" Jake asked.

"She should have answered that she wrote her biggest lie on her application form, that she was prepared to do anything to become an NSC officer.'

If the day had been difficult so far, things got increasingly competitive as the hours wore on. After the meal, the candidates who had passed the truth test were led into the gym again. I had tried to view the contest as being solely about my own abilities rather than the others. I liked Ruby from the start but was now resigned to her having to leave in order for me to win.

Jake was another matter. He was charm itself to the NSC officers and seemed to be popular with most of the other candidates. But there again, they hadn't seen the real Jake. I'd met him, though—the asshole lurking under the smiling mask.

In the gym, Commander Beecham ordered the remaining candidates to form a circle around a featureless mannequin, which he referred to as a Hand-to-Hand Combat Simulation Unit. Beecham explained that the Unit was programmed to train in several different forms of hand-to-hand combat, including Aikido, Tai Kwon Do, Kung Fu, and good old-fashioned street fighting. Once activated, the Unit could only be turned off by lethal blows applied to the Unit's throat, base of skull, or center of spine.

"Anything else," said Commander Beecham, "will only piss it off." So the object of this next test, he explained, was to defeat the Unit. Taking off his shirt to reveal an impressive physique, Beecham ordered the Unit to engage. On the command, its eyes glowed green.

"Karate," Beecham instructed the Unit, and they bowed to each other before snapping into karate stances. The Unit was the first to attack. It came at Beecham with a flurry of punches and kicks, each of which the commander expertly parried. Then Beecham went on the offensive, but all of his moves were blocked by the Unit. For several minutes, the fight went back and forth with neither seemingly able to land an effective blow. The end, though, came quite suddenly. Beecham feinted at the Unit's right and then skewed it with a punch to its throat. Instantly, the Unit's lights went out and it froze, defeated.

I watched the fight in fascination. The Unit was good, but Beecham was better, *much* better. I leaned forward and whispered under my breath to Ruby, "Talk about playing rough with your toys."

Ruby giggled quietly, as Beecham swung around to stare at her. "Something funny, Candidate?" he asked. "My demonstration amused you?"

Ruby reddened. "No, sir. Very impressive, sir," she said.

"Perhaps you want to impress your friends," Beecham said.

Ruby jumped up and snapped to attention. "No, sir. A candidate has no friends."

"Good answer," he said. "So let's see what you can do."

We watched as Ruby prepared to fight the Unit. "Street fighting," she told it. They both took their stances, their fists raised. Then Beecham ordered them to attack. The Unit jumped forward, punching with a right cross. Ruby just managed to dodge the vicious blow, but took a jab against her guard. She backed off, trying to work out how to get through to the Unit. It moved toward her and she retreated.

"Fight, woman! Don't run," Beecham ordered.

Ruby moved forward and tried to grab the machine, but it parried to the left and swung a fist towards the back of her head. I could see that it hurt Ruby. She tried to move away, but the Unit advanced on her. I saw panic in her eyes. The Unit struck out, once, twice, hard and fast into Ruby's midsection. She started to buckle as the machine moved closer.

Beecham shoved himself between Ruby and the Unit.

"Stop," he ordered, and the Unit froze.

"Sit down, Mason."

"But, sir, I can beat it. I know I can."

"I don't think so. Fail another test and you're out."

Shocked, Ruby sat down. I could see she was trying to hold back tears.

"Duran, you're up next."

I walked towards the machine slowly. This was going to be tough. As a cop, I'd had to fight drunks, big mouths, and gangbangers. I usually came out on top, but beating a robot designed to fight had to be different. I stared at the machine, giving it my best war-face. It simply looked back at me with blank eyes.

"Street fighting." I said to the Unit.

Its lights came on as I took a boxing stance and moved toward it. I lashed out, and it parried, blocking me. My hand hit metal. I pulled back and moved away. My fist stung.

I couldn't do that too often. We circled each other for a few moments before, suddenly, the Unit moved forward, punching me with a right cross.

I feinted left and grabbed at its arm, attempting to pull it forward, but it kicked out, smashing a steel foot into my knee. The pain was excruciating. My legs buckled, and I fell to the floor. The Unit raised its leg, ready to bring to bring it down on me, but I managed to crawl out of the way just in time.

Changing tactics, it reached out and grabbed my foot, flinging me up effortlessly. I landed hard on the wooden floor. Winded, I tried to get up as the Unit launched itself into the air. I rolled to the right, just managing to move out of the path of the descending steel fighter.

It hit the ground on its chest with a force that would have knocked the breath out of a normal person, but it did nothing to this machine. As I climbed to my feet, the Unit rose too. We stared at each other. While I was breathless and ached all over, the Unit looked completely unharmed.

This was impossible. How was I supposed to win?

The Unit advanced again, swinging its huge metal arms at me. I ducked and flipped back and into the air, my legs open. I scissor-gripped the head of the metal monster. The Unit fell with me on top, but not for long. It levered itself up as I quickly released my legs and used my arms to push away.

The Unit followed, crawling toward me, and brought its fist down hard, just missing my skull. I pulled my legs under my body and pushed with all my might. I thought I saw surprise in its face—or maybe I imagined it— as I jumped over its head onto its back, my weight forcing it down to floor face first. Elbowing the Unit's skull, I rolled it over as the lights of its eyes went out.

I stared down at the Unit. It lay motionless. I had won…barely.

Four more candidates took their chances with the machine, and Beecham had to disable it before it could do much damage to the first three—but for the fourth, his intervention came too late. The Unit managed to hit the unfortunate candidate hard on the back of his neck, and he fell to the floor, blood leaking from his ears.

Nobody moved. The room went silent as the candidate's body was stretchered out.

Commander Beecham was the first to speak. "That was an unfortunate incident, but you all signed agreements clearly stating that you could face injury or death when taking part in the candidate selection process. Any of you are, of course, free to leave at any point if you so desire."

He waited. No one moved.

"That's it for today. We start six a.m. sharp tomorrow morning."

CHAPTER SIX

AFTER OUR SECOND MEAL IN the canteen, which was once again a bizarre mixture of different foods, the remaining twenty-five candidates marched in single file through a labyrinth of corridors to reach a high-roofed, windowless room. A white-tiled wall separated the lower third section off from the rest of the room. This area, Commander Beecham explained, contained the latrines and washroom. Entry was through a large metal door. The rest of the room contained single beds.

We had five minutes before the lights were turned off, and we were expected to be washed, undressed, and in bed by then, ready to sleep. Anyone who was still up would be instantly failed, Commander Beecham told us. What's more, we were forbidden to talk from now on until the morning wake-up call.

Men and women rushed to complete their ablutions. Some opted to sleep naked. Others, like Ruby and I, remained partially dressed. Everyone concentrated on getting to bed on time. No one wanted to have to leave simply because they were still up. That would be incredibly stupid and pointless after the day we'd had.

Returning, Commander Beecham looked around. Satisfied that everyone was in bed, he repeated his warning that if anyone spoke or attempted any other form of communication or even left their beds for whatever reason during the night, they would be disqualified. I figured this was another test—this one designed to see who could or couldn't follow orders.

I saw no sign of any cameras, but I knew by now this didn't mean they didn't exist. I knew no one, myself included, was prepared to push the envelope. The remaining candidates only had one objective now—to win and become an officer.

I expected to go to sleep immediately after Commander Beecham left, but it was soon apparent this wasn't going to happen. I was exhausted, but my mind was still active. I kept going over what I could have done better and what might happen tomorrow. I had always been competitive, but these tests were making me unusually aggressive.

I stared around the dark room. Some people, the lucky ones, were already asleep. They would be well rested for tomorrow. Others, like me, remained awake. I closed my eyes and tried to will myself to sleep, but that didn't work. I worried if I really had what it took to be an NSC officer. I knew I had certain skills and abilities and training, but they would count for nothing if I couldn't continue to hack it mentally.

Maybe I wasn't strong enough. I had let Max down all those years ago, after all.

I prayed I wouldn't have the dream tonight.

With my eyes closed tight, I listened to the noises in the room. I heard fidgeting, rolling, snoring, the usual sounds that come from a group of sleeping adults.

Gradually, I drifted off to sleep.

It was the noise that woke me. It was low-pitched, distant—but growing closer. Another sound, slightly higher, cut across the droning sound. Something was familiar about it, and yet I struggled to identify either its exact source or work out what it was.

Then came a huge jolt, and the walls of the building shook. My bed started to move, sliding down towards the opposite wall. I could hear the other beds moving too.

Outside, the sounds became more agitated. The wall began to buckle. It moved in and out, backward and forward, and the noise outside grew louder and louder.

I squinted my eyes, trying to see anything that was happening, but the darkness was all-enveloping. I was aware of people moving, clearly awake, but heeding the words of Commander Beecham, no one spoke or made a sound.

I'm sure that they, like me, were trying to figure out if this was some kind of new test to discover who would panic and leave or start talking.

If it was, I was not going to fail. Suddenly my bed started to roll back and forth. The floor was buckling! I hung on tight as the noise outside became deafening.

It must be a test. It must be.

My bed was flung upward. I clung tight to it as my body bounced against the ceiling. The sounds from outside were louder and more insistent, the low-pitched hum fighting with the high-pitched whine, but I ignored them. I had other more important things to concentrate on, like not getting seriously hurt or even killed.

I held the side of my bed as its metal base twisted. It flipped, and I couldn't hold on anymore. I was hurtled out. I hit the floor, my hands outstretched to try and protect my face. I made a futile attempt to crawl away from my bed, which landed hard down on top of me, smashing my outstretched arm. The pain was excruciating.

All around, I could hear people shouting and screaming as they were flung from their moving beds. No one cared now if it was a test or not.

Then—silence. And the deep oblivion of unconsciousness.

The wailing Klaxon woke me. I yanked my head up off the pillow and stared around, remembering where I was.

I saw Ruby opening her eyes. Jake was awake too. Others were waking and looking around. Were they feeling like me? My body ached all over, and I felt like I had only slept for a few minutes.

The door slid open and Commander Beecham entered. "Candidates, you have five minutes before you leave, starting now."

Pandemonium broke loose as we all jumped out of bed.

"Oh, and talking is allowed now," Beecham said as he left the room, and we rushed to the sinks and toilets.

I found myself next to Ruby, who was splashing water on her face. "How'd you sleep?" I asked.

"Fine, I think. You?"

"Good. But not long enough." There was something nagging at the back of my mind. I looked at my arm. It had a huge bruise on it. When had that happened? I glanced over at Ruby. Her face looked puffy and there was a bruise under her eye.

She looked across at me. "War wound?" Ruby pointed at my arm.

"I guess. Must have got it yesterday. What about you?" I pointed at her face.

She put her hand up, feeling the bruise. "God knows how I got that. Those tests must have been tougher than I thought."

"Yeah. Another day, another dollar," I said as Ruby towel dried her face.

"I guess." She threw the towel down and headed out.

I forced myself to stay focused for the athletic tests, where the candidates' endurance was pushed to their limits, and I was aware that Ruby and Jake were still leading the pack, as was I. Then, after a brief meal, we were ordered to file out into an area at the back of the dome.

Now just fifteen of us were left, and we all were exhausted. The sun was starting to set over the horizon, and the camp was incredibly still as we checked out the large metal containers arranged in a single row in front of us. Each box was directly opposite a candidate.

"Attention," Commander Beecham ordered as General Stoker's glider ball whirred into view. This was a different man from the person we'd glimpsed when we'd first arrived. His voice was softer, less aggressive, and Stoker even congratulated us on being in the top three percent of all candidates.

"You have now come to your penultimate test," the general announced.

The glider ball floated over the line of boxes, and Stoker explained that each container would become a temporary home for one of us. We could stay in it for as long we liked, but during our time in The Box, we would receive no food or water. The moment you wanted to get out all you had to do was press the small button in the right corner of the box. The three who remained in their containers the longest would advance to the final selection. The rest would leave on the next transporter out.

It was Jake who asked the obvious question. "Sir? You'll relieve the final three, correct?"

General Stoker's stared at him. "You might be in there, wasting away, trying not to swallow your own tongue, considering drinking your own piss, but until you come out, you won't know if you're the first out or the last. My recommendation? Stay as long as you can, stay until you can't take another second—then stay some more!"

It was not the answer any of us wanted to hear.

As the glider ball zipped away, officers escorted us into our tiny prison boxes. I was ordered to take off all my clothes and my shoes before bending low to enter the container. Kneeling, I turned my head to take a last look out at the daylight as the door was pushed shut. No light came through the solid metal walls. I could barely stretch my arms and couldn't stand.

I moved around, trying to settle in one position. The Box seemed to have been designed to make you as uncomfortable as possible. I finally found the most bearable position: with my legs bent and my feet pushed up the wall, my back curved, and my hands outstretched. Crunched up in this pitch-black hellhole, I couldn't imagine I could stay put more than a few hours.

I stared out into the blackness and listened. Maybe I could hear something outside. But there was total silence. The Box must be completely soundproofed. With the darkness and the silence, it felt like I was floating.

Soon the toes on my left foot started to cramp. I scrunched them up and then released them. I did the same with the other foot. It seemed like I could feel every little muscle. I shut my eyes and tried to doze, but, as any insomniac knows, if your body doesn't want to sleep, it won't, no matter how exhausted you are.

After I'd completed National Service, I had taken a short meditation course to help me find out who I was and what I really wanted to do. But I soon discovered I wasn't a Zen kind of guy. Even still, I concentrated and tried to listen to my breathing. It was relaxing hearing the air coming in and out of my mouth. For a time, I almost forgot where I was until my butt started to itch. I tried to ignore it. It was probably psychosomatic. But the itch kept getting worse. I moved my backside from left to right, pulling it across the smooth steel floor. That felt better.

But it had broken the spell. Meditation was out. What now? Maybe I should think of something else? Anything. What about if I sang something? I realized that out of all the songs I had ever heard, I couldn't remember more than one line of lyrics from any of them.

What about when I was a kid? What was that song my mom used to sing to me?

I'm a little teapot, short and stout
Here's my handle, here's my spout
When I see the teacups, hear me shout
Tip me up and pour me out.

Incredible. After all these years, I could still remember the first verse word for word. Except for that third line. "When I see the teacups, hear me shout." Was that right? Maybe it was "When the water's boiling, hear me shout." No, that wasn't it. It was "When the kettle's boiling, hear me shout."

Or was it?

Then I felt a stabbing pain in my arm. What was that? I tried to move my arm but found myself rolling to the side, which put pressure on one of my legs, so I rolled back. At least the pain had gone now. This was crazy. How could anyone survive in here?

I closed my eyes again. Come on, *sleep*. Time to count sheep. I saw line upon line of the woolly animals jumping over a fence. I got up to two hundred. Shouldn't I be asleep now? Maybe I was? I opened my eyes. It was still pitch black and completely silent, and I was still awake!

And now I had to piss.

Should I? Just thinking about it made me want to do it even more. I felt the warm liquid trickle down my leg. That was better. Except the urine clung to my skin and I started to itch again. Forget it. It could be worse: I could be buried alive. I wondered how long anyone could survive in a coffin. Air would be the problem. Maybe three or four hours?

I started to breathe deeply. Was this a panic attack? *Calm down; you're not in a coffin.* They must have some sort of oxygen recycling system, right? It was just a test. They wouldn't kill me. Would they? Just what were they testing now? I was losing it.

My eyes got heavy and closed. The outside world felt remote and slowly fell away.

I turned. I was staring into a store window filled with cakes. They were all different colors and sizes. I'd never felt so hungry. I wanted to go in but couldn't, somehow. Something was wrong with my feet. It seemed as if they had melted into the ground. Now what was happening to the floor? It was morphing, melting from a concrete sidewalk to a tarmac road to an open parade ground where new police recruits lined up in front of a long, high podium. I looked down. I was wearing my police uniform. I stared up at the podium. A banner floated in the air. I tried to read the words, but I couldn't make them out. And people were laughing. What was happening?

The cops had disappeared. I was walking along the sidewalk, a gun holster and belt strapped around my waist. People were pointing at me. Why were they all looking? I glanced down. I was naked, and so was the man walking with me. I knew him. I knew his name. Max. There was a shot. Max fell. I tried to run to him, but someone pulled me back. I had to get out. I had to go.

As my hands reached out, they touched cold steel. It was Max's wheelchair, right in front of me. "Hang in there, buddy," Max said. I blinked hard, and he was gone. Then I saw a blinding white flash—

And suddenly I woke, opening my eyes wide.

Every part of my body ached. I tried to stretch and move, but it was as if I was frozen. I stared at my hand and willed my fingers to move. They bent forward and back. I pushed out my legs, felt pins and needles shoot through them. I levered myself hard against the steel wall. I lifted my arm and moved it back, for the first time smelling something. What was that? I wrinkled my nose and tried to hold back the vomit building in my throat. Shit and urine. Everything about me and around me *reeked* of shit and urine. Now I wanted to retch, but nothing came up. How long had I been here? I tried to focus. What had he said? Even when you think you want to come out, don't. Stay longer.

But I couldn't.

I opened my mouth to scream, but only a feeble croak came out. I slammed my hand hard against the metal wall. It made a low dull sound. Useless. No one could hear that. I moved my head to the left and right and then as far around as possible. Wait. Hadn't Beecham mentioned a button in the right corner? I bent forward, trying to find it. It couldn't be more than inches away. I pushed hard with my legs, pulling my body up and twisting. Now my hand was closer. I was almost there. Summoning all of my strength, I finally felt it, then pressed the tip of my finger on it and waited.

After what seemed like an eternity, the heavy metal door behind me slid open a few inches. A voice came from outside. "Cover your eyes, Candidate." I reached up to cup my hands around my face. The metal door slid open further, and I jammed my feet through. Bright sunlight streamed in, and as I opened my eyes, I saw an unfocused figure standing in front of me, looking down.

"Here, Candidate. Put these on," the voice ordered. I grabbed at the pair of sunglasses and pushed them on. Commander Beecham? I could see now. Yes, it was the commander. He stood over me, offering an open canteen of water and a blanket to wrap around me. I grabbed at the container and took one swig, then another. I wanted to drink forever.

Beecham snatched the canteen back. "That's enough."

"How long?"

"Twenty-seven hours."

"Did I make it?"

An undefinable expression crawled across the man's face. I waited. So did he. At last he shook his head. "Sorry, pal."

CHAPTER
SEVEN

I N THE CANTEEN, THE NSC officers sat at tables, talking and eating The serving hatches were open. Officers stood ahead of me as I waited in line for food. It had been two hours since I'd come out of The Box, and I felt almost normal. But I was still finding it impossible to accept that this was it, the end of my journey. I had failed.

Ruby and Jake had both made it. Ironically, they had only stayed in their boxes a matter of minutes more. We had all been inside the tiny containers for just over a day, but unlike me, they had been taken away to complete the final test that would decide which of them would become an NSC officer.

After getting out, I had been escorted to the shower room where I'd relished the sensation of the water pummeling my body and the dirt and grime being washed off. I had drunk a little more water, but so far had only been allowed a snack bar as I'd been warned I should wait. Now I was ravenous

I finally reached the end of the line. I held out my tray and a server threw thick slices of white meat onto my plate. I had no idea what it was. Resisting the temptation to snatch it up and gulp it down immediately, I simply stared at the food.

"What's that?"

"Turkey" the server said. "For Thanksgiving."

Thanksgiving? That was something I had completely forgotten. In the outside world, it really wasn't that important anymore. Just being able to survive day-to-day was enough to celebrate.

"Since most of the officers are about to go on leave, I put it out today," the server said as I leaned forward to smell the white slices. It didn't appear to be synthetic, but surely it couldn't be real?

"Real turkey meat. From a real turkey," she confirmed.

I vaguely remembered eating turkey when I was younger, but that must have been the last time I'd tasted it. Taking my meal to an empty seat, I sat down and, despite my hunger, slowly ate the meat.

As I chewed, I reflected. Here I was, savoring the most delicious meal I'd had in years, given to me courtesy of the NSC canteen. But I was never coming back here. My life was about to go to shit all over again.

I looked across at the officers, chatting with each other without a care in the world. They were happy to go home, and I was certain that their Thanksgiving celebrations were going to be way, way better than mine. I watched as a group of them stood up to leave, passing Commander Beecham as he entered the canteen.

The commander went to the serving hatch, collected a tray of food, and took a seat at an empty table close by. He started eating, keeping his eyes down and staring at his plate.

And suddenly, I got angry. *Really* angry. He knew I was here, yet he chose to ignore me. In his eyes I suppose I was just another failed candidate, someone he wanted nothing to do with. Of course, I knew it was never more than an outside chance I would win the coveted officer position, but the longer the tests went on, the more confident I had become. I could have done it. I know I could.

I pushed back my chair, stood up rapidly, and walked over to the commander. "Sir, can we talk?"

"I'm eating." Beecham didn't look up.

Ignoring this, I sat opposite. "Yes, sir, and I'm going back to the city because I failed one small test by a matter of minutes. I don't think that's fair."

Beecham cut into a slice of turkey and jabbed at it with his fork. "Do you think that life was fair for this creature, Duran?"

"With respect, sir, I'm not a piece of meat."

"Tell that to a lion. We're all animals, Duran, and we have to accept what fate doles out to us."

"Well, I don't accept it. I *won't* accept it, sir. I believe I am an ideal candidate and would make an excellent NSC officer, just as good as any of those men over there." I pointed to the other officers in the canteen.

Beecham put down his knife and fork and looked up at me. "The decision wasn't just made on The Box results."

"What?"

"The brain scan indicated some…worrying traits."

I stared at him, thinking back to how the medic had consulted with Beecham before he had told me to go.

"You almost failed me then?"

Beecham smiled. "You remember, now, do you, Candidate?" He paused. "Before joining the police force, you were in the military, right?"

"Yes, sir. National Service. Like everyone else."

"And you fought in the Albanian War?"

"Yes, sir."

"And yet, when you were offered the chance to join the army after your National Service ended, you turned it down. Correct?"

I nodded. The NSC had obviously thoroughly vetted me.

"Why didn't you take the opportunity to serve your country, Duran?"

"With respect, sir, I didn't see it that way. I wanted time to decide what to do with my life."

"And after a few years of doing very little, you joined the police force."

"Yes, sir."

"Which you left a few years ago because of an incident with your partner. He was shot?"

"I don't see what this has to do with anything."

"According to your scan, you have a problem sticking with things. You don't like commitment. You lack determination."

"Leaving the police had nothing to do with determination. It had everything to do with—" I stopped.

"Guilt? And what about your military service—or lack of it?"

"I served with distinction, sir. I received a Medal of Honor. You can't accuse me of not serving my country." I was furious now. "You have to allow me to complete the tests. I'm exactly who you are looking for, sir."

Beecham stared at me. "Are you now?"

"Yes, sir." I stared at him defiantly.

He smiled. "Well done, Duran. *Finally*. That's what we've been wanting from you. Something that showed us what you really thought about your abilities and a real indication that faced with rejection and adversity, you would fight on." He stopped. "Very well—you're in again."

"What?"

"I said I am going to give you a second chance, Candidate. Don't waste it."

I smiled broadly. "Thank you, sir. Thank you very much."

Beecham stood. "We had to be sure, you know."

"What? This was some sort of test?"

"Right in one, Duran. You've got the third slot. Report to the Virtual Reality Room in half an hour. Stay there and an officer will come to get you."

Beecham started to walk away.

"Sir, one thing. What's the VRC test about?"

"Can't help you on that, Candidate, but remember anything that happens in there happens out here. So if you get hurt there, you will really get hurt. Good luck," he said. "Oh, and by the way, you know Mason was in the same regiment in Albania as you? A few years later, of course. Small world, isn't it?" Beecham said before heading for the door.

We stood to attention when the steel door of the VCR Room slid open and Commander Beecham entered.

Ruby, Jake, and I had been waiting for Beecham's arrival for five minutes, nervous about what lay ahead. We already knew this was the final test, though none of us could guess what it involved. But after completion we were aware only one of us would be given the chance to become an NSC officer. The others would return to the city and that would be devastating.

"At ease, Candidates." Beecham walked across and handed each of us a pair of goggles.

"When I give the order, you will put these eye glasses on. You will then enter the virtual scenario we have chosen for you. There you have each been given a quad bike. On these and in the backpacks by the vehicles, you will find maps, weapons, explosives, and rock-climbing equipment. A separate backpack contains a very important package. It is the team's mission to deliver this to the coordinates marked on the maps. Is this clear?"

"Yes, sir," we chorused.

"Okay. Goggles on, Candidates," Beecham ordered.

I slipped the strap of the glasses over the back of my head, pulling them down to cover my eyes.

The world seemed to shrink and fall away. And then—

And then I stood in a thick blanket of snow. Tall redwoods surrounded me, their branches flecked by a light dusting of white. In the distance I glimpsed snow-covered mountains, high to the north and low to the south. I squeezed the down jacket I was now wearing and leaned against my quad bike. Ruby and Jake stood to my left next to their vehicles, dressed for the cold weather. They, too, were taking in this new world. It all looked incredible—and utterly, irrevocably real.

After two days of tests that had stretched us to our limits and beyond, this mission sounded straightforward and fun. It was also good to work as a team, even if that team included Jake.

Commander Beecham suddenly appeared in front of us. "One more detail you should know," he said. "There are men chasing you for the package. Do not let them get it!"

He vanished—and I heard the distant sound of racing engines.

We were traveling downhill fast, swerving around the trees as the quad bikes appeared over the brow of the hill.

I crouched low, my own quad bike bouncing along the snow-covered ground. I reached behind me to steady my backpack and prevent it from swinging forward. Then, glancing around, I checked out the pursuing bikes. Ten of them, about a quarter mile back.

One quad accelerated away from the pursuing pack and, pulling out his gun, the driver fired at us. Ruby spun around to shoot back. Her third bullet struck him, but just as he fell to the ground, his final shot found its target, slamming into the engine of Ruby's bike. She clung on, desperately trying to retain control of the vehicle, but it was no use. The quad swerved on its side and headed directly for a massive redwood tree. Hitting the trunk, Ruby was thrown off, falling heavily onto the ground.

Seeing this, I shouted across to Jake. "Explosives!"

Jake shook his head and pointed to my backpack. "Swap!"

I pulled the backpack off and threw it across to Jake. He reached down to his saddlebag and yanked out a small plastic bottle filled with a blue liquid. He moved his quad close to mine and tossed the container over. I caught it with one hand.

Jake drove on as I swung my bike around and headed back to Ruby, who was rising shakily to her feet. "Get on my bike!" I shouted to her as I dismounted. "I'll be right back." Then I ran up to her crashed vehicle and carefully placed the plastic bottle and its liquid contents under it. I looked up to see Ruby frantically waving.

"Come on! Come on!" she shouted.

I glanced behind. Our pursuers were getting close.

Ruby opened up the bike's throttle as shots rang out behind us. I jumped onto the quad, pushed up close to Ruby, and put my hand over her hand. "Drive slowly," I ordered as I pulled out my gun.

"What?"

"Just do it."

The pursuers had almost reached us as Ruby edged the quad bike forward. I fired. My bullet tore through the center of the plastic container. The explosion lifted the disabled bike up and smashed it into the giant tree.

"Go!" I shouted.

Ruby opened the throttle, and the quad bike shot away.

I looked back. The huge tree was swaying backward and forward as the first pursuing rider reached it. He glanced up and wildly accelerated, but it was too late. The tree fell with a crash, crushing the rider flat.

Behind him, the rest of the chasing pack broke hard, desperate to avoid plowing into the fallen redwood. But they couldn't stop in time. Their quad bikes smashed into the tree, and they were thrown high into the sky.

Ruby twisted around. "I don't think they'll be bothering us again." She grinned.

Then, with me clinging on the back, she expertly gunned the engine and headed after Jake.

By the time we caught up with him, Jake had come to a halt in front of an almost-vertical cliff face and was pulling out climbing gear from his pannier.

"Let's go," he said. "We've got to keep moving."

"And nice to see you too," Ruby muttered as she climbed off her quad.

But Jake was right. This was no time for pleasantries. We didn't know who else was programmed to come after us, and according to the map coordinates we'd been given, scaling the rock face would take us to the exit matrix.

We pulled straws to decide our climbing order. Jake would lead, then me, with Ruby behind. Jake also insisted he continued to carry the all-important backpack, and rather than waste time arguing, we let him.

We decided to be roped together, so if anyone lost their footing, the others could stop them from falling. We would use our grappling hooks to cut into the cliff face and pull ourselves up.

Climbing the sheer precipice was painstakingly slow and required total concentration. After an hour of strenuous work, Jake had almost reached the top. He pulled a grappling reel from his belt and fired it into the air. It passed the summit and dug deep into the ground above the cliff face.

That's when he made his move.

It happened so fast: I heard a sawing sound directly above me, and almost before I could look up, Jake had cut through the towrope with a long, serrated knife he'd produced from God knows where. "Ruby!" I screamed as I dug my fingers into a crack in the face of the cliff. Below me, Ruby swung in towards the rock, lost her footing, and bounced out again, almost pulling me off my handholds.

I looked up to see Jake hit a switch on the grappling hook and reel himself to safety. Swinging his backpack around, he dropped it to the ground beside him.

"You son of a bitch!" I desperately pulled myself into the rock face, clinging tight to the cliff face. I looked down. Somehow, Ruby had managed to get a hand and foothold in the rocks.

"You okay?" I shouted down.

"Yeah, but Hogan, we'll have to climb without ropes. I'll cut you free from me, okay?"

"Go ahead."

Ruby used a knife to slice through the climbing rope. From now on, we were on our own.

It took about another twenty minutes to inch my way up, but finally I reached the summit. Using my full arm-strength, I dragged my body over the crest and slumped down. But I only rested momentarily. Moving to lean over the clifftop, I offered my open hands to Ruby. Grasping them, she pulled herself up to join me. As we both slumped down, relieved and exhausted, a burst of static filled the air.

"SIMULATION OVER," boomed a computerized voice.

Instantly the cliff face disappeared.

I took off my goggles. Ruby and I were back in the VR Room. General Stoker in the flesh stood on the opposite side of the room. He had obviously been waiting for us.

"Well done, Mason and Duran," General Stoker said. "Unfortunately, though...not good enough."

"Sir, Teerman cut our climbing rope. He sabotaged us," Ruby said.

"Yes—and effective immediately, Candidate Jacob Teerman is a National Security Council officer. I've already released him to make preparations to leave."

We stared at the general, not believing what we'd just heard.

"He *won?*" I said, astonished.

"After what he did?" Ruby said.

"An NSC officer is loyal to his mission first, his comrades second. You all had one mission. Deliver the package at any cost. Teerman did that. He took the package from you, Duran, and brought it to the clifftop. Commander Beecham will see to it that you two get the next transporter back to the city." Stoker turned to leave. "That's the way things are here." He looked over his shoulder at us. "Teerman knew that from day one. Why didn't you?"

CHAPTER EIGHT

TWO TRANSPORTERS WERE PARKED AT the front of the complex. NSC personnel filed onto them. Ruby and I walked toward the last of the vehicles. We were too upset to speak.

I tried to psych myself up, convince myself that this wasn't the end of the world. Except it was. It was the second time that I'd been told I'd failed, and I guess I expected another miracle. Instead, Ruby and I were marched out of the fortress.

I stole a glance over at Ruby. She, too, had come so close and had passed every test, except this last one. Her expression was unreadable, but I could only imagine she was thinking the same things I was.

An NSC officer stepped forward and blocked our path as we reached the transporter.

"NSC only," he snarled. "Civilians ride up top." The man pointed to a ladder at the side of the vehicle that led up to the roof.

"You can't be serious," I said.

"I said, *up top*," the officer repeated.

I looked across at Ruby. What choice did we have? We climbed up the narrow ladder to the transporter roof. It was flat and enclosed by a metal railing.

"What are you going to do now?" Ruby asked.

I shrugged. I really didn't know. We sat in silence for a few moments. Then: "Apparently, you were in the same regiment as me in Albania."

"You were in the Second Battalion?"

I nodded. "Yeah."

"I should never have left. Best years of my life."

"Come on, Ruby, you're not that old. Plenty of time left yet."

"What, as a stripper?"

"Of course not, but…"

"But what?"

"I was just going to ask, why did you leave the army?"

"Greed. I got a great job offer from one of the big tech companies. They wanted me to use the computer skills I learned in the army. It was fantastic at first, but being a woman…" She stopped. "Well, it got to the point where the only way to get on was to sleep my way up to the top, something I wasn't prepared to do. So my boss fired me and put the word around that I wasn't up to it. Never got any work in the industry after that. In fact, getting any work *at all* was difficult. You may not believe it, but as a stripper, I at least kept my dignity." She stopped and pointed. "Hey, here they come."

We watched as Jake and General Stoker walked toward a limousine. They climbed into the vehicle, and it accelerated to the front of the convoy. Our transporter started up and we held tight to the rail as it moved forward to take its place behind the other transporter. A large armored truck pulled behind us, its engine running.

"Where are all these people going?" Ruby asked.

I explained what the cook had said about Thanksgiving.

"People still celebrate Thanksgiving?" Ruby said.

"Those that have something to be thankful for."

Ahead, the main gates slowly opened, and with the limo leading, the convoy exited into the barren wasteland beyond. Looking back, I saw the gates close rapidly. Just a day before, I had seen them open for the first time.

In the wasteland, nothing moved. Anyone with any sense wasn't going to venture out in this heat. The vehicles in the convoy increased their speed as they bounced along the road, whipping up dust in their wakes.

"You know, I learned something important in there," Ruby shouted over the noise of the engine.

"What's that?" I shouted back.

"Although I might not have what it takes to be an NSC officer, I know that I have what it takes to be a better person than them."

I smiled at her and was about to reply when I was distracted by something flashing in the hills ahead.

"Did you see that?" I asked.

"What?"

There was another flash from up high.

"There," I said, pointing up to the hills. It looked like the sun was flashing off something. A mirror—or the lens of a pair of binoculars.

Ruby shook her head. "I don't see anything."

She was right. I couldn't see anything up there now, either.

I stared ahead. Was that a tunnel running through the hills? Were we going home a different way? When we'd arrived, I didn't recall traveling through anything like that. I returned my gaze to the hills but saw no sign of whoever was watching us.

In a couple of minutes, the lead vehicle, the limo, entered the tunnel. The front transporter was next in, followed by our vehicle. The armored truck played shotgun at the back.

It was pitch black inside. Way ahead, a tiny pinpoint of light signaled the exit. I felt the hairs on the back of my neck stand up.

Something wasn't right.

Suddenly, from up front came the sound of an explosion that sent rocks and debris crashing down, blocking the tunnel's exit.

"What the—?" I exclaimed as our transporter juddered to a halt. And out of the blackness came shouting, screaming Krails who rolled small metal balls under the vehicles.

Ruby and I hurled ourselves off the transporter roof to safety. But it was too late for the men and women in the vehicles. They didn't stand a chance as the metal balls exploded and pressure-cooked them all inside the transport.

I pushed against the tunnel's brick wall, raising my arm to my eyes to protect them from the searing heat of the explosion. Through the billowing smoke and flames, I glimpsed Krails surrounding the limo. Some pressed their faces hard against its tinted windows. Others bashed their fists and clubs against the car and started to rock it backward and forward.

I saw the huge Krail I had spotted on our arrival slowly walk toward the limo, ignoring the mayhem all around him. He raised his hand, and the other Krails moved away from the vehicle.

As all the attention was focused on the limousine, I yanked open the transporter door and pulled two guns out of the holsters of the dead driver and guard. Throwing one weapon to Ruby, I pointed to the armored truck that had stopped at the entrance to the tunnel. "Let's hitch a ride."

Ruby nodded. "Good idea."

We ran toward the vehicle. But the armored truck driver had already decided what he needed to do. He reversed at high speed, mowing down Krails trying to block his exit. Others jumped on the truck, holding on tight. But the driver slammed on the brakes, and all but one of the Krails were flung off. The remaining Krail, a small, wiry redhead, clung tight to the roof.

The armored truck swung around and headed back down the highway as Ruby and I ran out of the tunnel. A bike-riding Krail spotted us. With one hand steering the cycle, the Krail used his other hand to swing a large spiked ball on a metal chain around his head. He powered the bike straight towards me.

"Move! Move!" Ruby screamed as the bike shot forward. But I stood my ground, resisting the urge to run. As the bike barreled toward me, I realized it may have been a stupid decision to stay, but now it was too late to bolt. I pulled out my gun and unloaded the weapon into the head and chest of the bike rider, blowing him backward off the motorcycle.

The rider-less bike continued on. I sidestepped the machine and tried to jump onto the cycle's seat, like a cowboy mounting a moving horse, except it wasn't that easy! I slipped and almost fell off before managing to clutch the handlebars. Then I swung the bike around.

"Get on," I shouted to Ruby, who was looking nervously at other Krails running toward her. She leapt onto the back of the bike, and I threw the cycle into gear, kicking dust into the faces of the pursuing Krails.

Head down, with Ruby clinging on tight, I chased after the armored truck. Ahead I could see that the redheaded Krail had managed to stay on the roof of the truck and was crawling from the back toward the front of the vehicle.

The Krail turned, spotted my bike, and waved his hands, signaling the others. Two of them pulled their motorcycles around and headed to cut me off. I slowed, and Ruby waited until the riders were almost upon us. Then she twisted and fired, shooting first one and then the other with unerring accuracy.

Accelerating again, I managed to pull the bike up and run parallel with the armored truck. From here I could see that the driver was frantically shouting into his radio, calling for help.

As I pulled the bike closer to the truck, the redheaded Krail swung down to hang from the roof and peer through the vehicle's side window. He stuck a small black cylinder on the glass, before pulling himself back up onto the roof.

I swerved away as a huge blast broke the window into a hundred shards that flew toward the driver, cutting his flesh to ribbons and covering his face with blood. One larger glass sliver drove hard into the base of the driver's neck and through to the other side, and he fell dead to the cabin floor.

Swinging back down, the Krail reached through the broken window, and opened the door. Jumping in, he yanked the dead driver out of the truck, and climbed into the driver's seat.

I swerved to avoid the body as it fell to the ground. "Ruby!" I shouted. "Take the bike and pull alongside."

She leaned forward to grasp the handlebars. I leapt from the bike and grabbed the truck's side window, clumsily dropping my pistol. Cursing at my stupidity, I pushed my hand hard through the window, and tried to punch the redheaded Krail. But he ducked, reached for his gun, and fired. I swung to the side to avoid getting shot.

Levering back, I grabbed the Krail's wrist and pulled it hard against the broken side window. The glass cut deep into the man's hand and, as blood spurted out, the Krail dropped his weapon out of the truck and pulled his hand back in. I climbed through the window and grabbed him, slamming his head hard onto the steering wheel.

The Krail ignored the pain and leaned down to retrieve a black-handled hunting knife from his boot. Pulling his arm up, he pushed the knife forward, stabbing at me again and again. I twisted my body around, narrowly avoiding being cut to pieces.

Ruby accelerated and pulled her bike up parallel to the truck. "Hogan! Catch!" She tossed her gun through the window. I caught the weapon, pulled back the safety, and pointed it at the Krail. "Drop the knife," I ordered.

The Krail grinned and raised the dagger. "Don't bother," I said. "You'll be dead before you move."

The Krail shrugged. "You win." He let the weapon drop to the floor, and I hit him hard, coldcocking him. Then I yanked him out of the driver's seat, pushing him onto the passenger side. Climbing over the unconscious Krail, I grabbed the truck's steering wheel to take control of the careering vehicle.

Outside, Ruby had climbed onto the seat of the bike. She jumped and grabbed the vehicle's side window to pull herself through. As she did, the bike spun away. Climbing in, Ruby wiped her bloodied hands on the unconscious Krail. I handed her the gun.

"Cover him," I said.

Behind us was the sound of gunfire. Glancing into the side mirror, I saw a single bike gaining on us fast. It was the huge Krail leader. He held the handlebars with one hand and a massive gun in the other, shooting at the truck as he drove.

In the distance, the NSC complex came into view. I scrambled for the radio, slipping the headset over my head.

"This is Candidate forty-five, forty-five dash nine calling. Let us in, now."

The dispatch officer sounded unimpressed. "Prove it," he said.

"Jeez. My guess is the NSC would want you to get whatever the heck is being carried in this truck to safety," I replied. "You can let us in or we're going through the gate regardless—full speed ahead." There was a long silence as I continued to drive at full speed, straight for the main gates. I got closer and closer, praying they would open.

The radio finally crackled. "Opening, Candidate."

I saw that the gates had started to move and glanced in the side mirror. The big Krail had almost caught up to us.

Ruby looked across anxiously as the Krail drew parallel to the driver's door. He smiled and lifted his gun to aim at my head. I snapped the door open. The Krail couldn't stop quickly enough. He slammed headfirst into it.

The Krail's bike skidded sideways along the ground, throwing up dust and rocks. My vehicle hurtled on as the big Krail slowly got to his feet and let out a blood-curdling war cry.

We were now almost at the gates, which had still to fully open. "We're not going to make it!" Ruby shouted.

I looked into the side mirror again. More bike-riding Krails were speeding toward the NSC complex and a rocket was zipping through the air toward us.

With only inches to spare, I threaded the needle through the gates as the missile flew over the truck and hit one of the towers inside the base. It exploded on contact, blasting a huge hole into the steel structure.

Inside the fortress, I braked hard, pulling to a halt beside a tow truck. Behind us, the gates were almost closed, but the Krails were still accelerating.

"Ruby, the gates!" I jumped out of the vehicle and ran toward the tow truck. Grabbing a roll of wire and a pair of thick gloves from the back of the vehicle, I sprinted to Ruby.

The gates were almost closed now, but the narrow gap gave the two lead Krail bikers just enough space to squeeze through. As they headed for us, we separated to stand about ten yards apart. I wore one of the tow truck gloves. Ruby had the other on. We held the tow wire between us.

"Now!" I separated farther to pull the wire taut as the bikers accelerated. They saw the cable, but it was too late. They both hit the wire at the same time.

It severed their heads from their bodies, and their bikes smacked into the side of the armored truck. Behind us, the gates finally closed.

Running, Commander Beecham and four NSC officers appeared from around the corner, their guns drawn. "What the hell's going on?" Beecham yelled.

"Ambush. Dozens of Krails," I said.

"Everyone else is dead," Ruby added. "At least that's what it looks like."

"Everyone?"

"Except for the Krail we captured. He's in the armored truck."

I led Beecham and the officers over to the armored truck's cab, climbed up the steps, and pulled open the door. The Krail was just coming around. He raised his head as he saw me. "Come on out," I ordered. Scowling, he dropped to the ground and stared at the NSC officers who covered him with their guns.

"What's your name, son?" Beecham asked.

"I ain't your son," the Krail growled.

"Whatever your name is, these men will be taking you to your new home." Beecham nodded to the officers, who pushed the scowling Krail forward.

"Move," one of them ordered.

"What about Jerry?" Beecham asked as we watched the captured prisoner and the NSC officers disappear around the corner.

"Jerry?" I looked over at Ruby. "Who the heck's Jerry?"

Beecham didn't answer, but instead walked to the back of the armored truck and pressed a red intercom button. He spoke into the small speaker grill. "Jerry—you all right in there?"

Ruby and I exchanged glances. We had no idea someone was in the back of the vehicle. A disembodied voice came back through the small speaker. "I...I am neither authorized nor able to open this truck from the inside. I have food and water enough to sustain—"

"Jerry, it's Beecham. You're back at base. Can you open up?"

"How do I know this is really Commander Beecham?" Jerry asked.

"I'm the one who didn't punish you for sneaking that young prostitute in here." Beecham winked at us.

There was a long silence. Then: "So, what happened out there, Commander?"

The commander looked across at us. "Tell him."

"Jerry, this is Candidate forty-five, forty-five dash nine. Hogan Duran. We were ambushed by Krails and, except for you, Candidate Ruby Mason, and me, everyone else was killed."

"Including Dad?"

"Who?"

"I'm afraid it's looking like the general is dead too," Commander Beecham interjected.

"General Stoker is his father?" I whispered to Beecham, who nodded.

From inside the truck there was an even longer silence.

"Jerry, you still there?" Commander Beecham asked.

"I was thinking about my father."

Silence again.

"Jerry?"

"Sorry."

We could hear the man was quietly crying.

"You okay?"

"You sure he's dead?"

Beecham looked at Ruby and me. "No, we're not—not absolutely," said Ruby.

"Yeah, you know your father. Toughest man on the planet. It would take more than a few Krails to kill him," Commander Beecham said.

"Yeah, that's what I think too." Jerry sniffled. "That's not going to happen."

He went quiet again.

"Jerry?" said Commander Beecham.

"Sorry, I was thinking that without my dad here, I've got a problem. This truck has an I-Lock. It needs my iris ID and fingerprint inside and an authorizer's iris ID and fingerprint outside. In LA there are ten authorizers. But out here there's only one: my dad. There's no other way for me to get out."

Commander Beecham frowned. "Okay. Sit tight, Jerry, we'll figure something out." He motioned Ruby and I to walk away from the truck.

"So he's stuck in the truck?" I asked.

"For now," said Beecham. "How certain are you that the general is dead?"

"It didn't look good out there, Commander."

"That's what I figured. And we have an even bigger problem. The missile you dodged struck our coms tower. We're silenced for a while—no way to send out for reinforcements."

"That's bad news."

"There is some *good* news, though," Beecham added. "We're still perfectly safe in here. We just have to sit tight. And that goes for Jerry too."

He stopped as a glider ball flew into view and hovered close by. Inside the ball, we could see the face of a pretty, but obviously worried, woman. "You better get over to the mainframe right now, sir." The woman spoke directly to Commander Beecham. "We have a problem."

CHAPTER NINE

A HANDSOME WOMAN IN HER TWENTIES and dressed in large, unflattering coveralls walked rapidly through the mainframe room toward us. She was the woman we'd seen in the glider ball. She looked pissed. "What are you two doing in here?" She pointed at Ruby and me. "This room's for authorized personnel only."

"I'm authorizing them," Beecham said. "Now, Rodriguez, what was so urgent?"

The woman pulled out a small, black plastic box from one of her numerous coverall pockets and touched the monitor on its front. A screen appeared, floating in mid-air. It showed five dual-colored bars, each with a percentage meter in the center, and in each, this percentage was down in the upper eighties or low nineties. "See?" she said, pointing at the display.

"See what, Rodriguez?" Beecham asked.

"The system is being hacked."

"So? Why don't you simply follow protocol and run the diagnostic?"

"I'm a systems operator. That's a job for a systems *maintainer*."

I expected this. At a time when so few had jobs, protecting them through increased specialization had become the norm. The plus was that people became more skilled in their limited field. The downside was that now people typically knew virtually nothing about anything outside of their specific expertise.

"I can do it, sir," Ruby said quickly.

"Sure, you can," said Rodriguez sarcastically. She gestured around the room. "These four walls contain some of the most sophisticated computer technology in the world. Do you even have a COM phone?"

"Get her a Mac series three thousand tablet, and she'll show you how she can block the attacking hacker," I said quickly and smiled at Ruby. "You *do* have one of those available, don't you, Rodriguez?"

Commander Beecham looked from Rodriguez to Ruby. "Can you really do this?"

"Yes, sir. I was trained as a software engineer and analyst when I was in the army."

Commander Beecham smiled. "Excellent, Ruby. Okay, Rodriguez, get her the equipment."

But Rodriguez made a face. "She'll need clearance, sir."

The commander shrugged. "Organize it, then."

Rodriguez sighed deeply before sending a silver glider ball off to retrieve the Mac. It returned moments later, its front snapping open to reveal the requested tablet. Ruby grabbed the computer and started typing rapidly.

Rodriguez and Commander Beecham exchanged glances. There was no doubt that the woman knew what she was doing. After only a few moments, Ruby looked up from her work. "Do you want the good or the bad news?"

"Just tell me what's going on, Candidate. No games," Beecham said irritably.

"The bad news is I haven't found a way to break through the communications cloak that the Krails have around this whole complex. However, the good news is, I *have* removed the malware that the hacker used to enter the mainframe. So for the time being, the danger to the system has been averted."

I was impressed, of course, but I didn't much like one of the phrases she used. "For the time being?" What exactly did that mean?

"The defenses I set up should hold the Krail hackers back for about three hours, possibly longer. I can try a few other things, too, that may extend that timeline," Ruby said.

I sighed and pulled a face. Rodriguez looked over at me. "What's with you? You do realize that the three hours she got us is much more than we could have hoped for. Good work, Ruby."

"Sorry." I glanced across at the commander. He had remained quiet.

A glider ball floated into view and headed for Beecham. Reaching him, the ball's screen flicked on and a spotty, lank-haired twenty-year-old stared out. "Anderson in observation, sir. You'd better come see this."

Beecham shook his head. What more could go wrong?

Commander Beecham and I left Ruby and Rodriguez in the mainframe room setting up the computer defenses. We headed along a series of narrow corridors, following the glider ball to the observation tower. On the way, I quizzed Beecham about who was still on the base and when we could expect help.

The commander didn't hold back. "There's no way to sugar coat this, Duran. We only have a skeleton crew remaining. The rest have left for the holidays. The last of those were with you, on the ambushed transporters. They weren't even due in LA for a couple more hours. When they don't turn up, the NSC will try and contact us, which of course they won't be able to do. So..." He hesitated. "We're talking about a minimum of six hours before we can expect assistance."

Six hours, and the system could be taken over in three.

Commander Beecham added one last nugget of depressing information. As it was a holiday, headquarters might simply send out a small maintenance crew who, of course, could be wiped out by the Krails on their way over.

I digested the information. My life had gone on a complete rollercoaster journey in the past forty-eight hours—from a high, when I got the news about being accepted as an NSC candidate, to a low when I had been told I had failed the training and had to go home. Then there had been the chaos of the ambush and our escape, which had seemed good news until now.

There was a real chance none of us would be able to get out of here alive.

The sound of a sliding door opening brought me out of my reverie. We had reached the observation tower.

CHAPTER TEN

O N MY ARRIVAL AT THE base I had seen the metal-clad observation tower from the outside. It was one of the two buildings adjacent to the fortress and perched high above it.

The room we entered was circular, its walls built out of tinted armored glass. A row of swivel chairs sat in its center. A skinny, callow youth was perched cross-legged on one of these. He swung his chair around as Beecham and I entered, stood to attention, saluted, and introduced himself as NSC Anderson.

Beecham got straight down to business. "Well? What is it Anderson?"

The observation officer turned to stare out of the window at the wasteland beyond. "There. That's the problem." He indicated outside.

Beecham and I peered out. We could see nothing.

"Anderson, you're forgetting your implants. We can't see through the wall like you. So what exactly are we looking at?"

Anderson shrugged and clicked his fingers twice, and a grid appeared on the glass in front of us. He reached out to touch one of the grid marks. The other grids peeled away and the mark expanded to fill the glass wall. Now Commander Beecham and I could see what, for Anderson, was already perfectly obvious.

Jake Teerman and General Stoker were perched high on a hill, their arms and legs outstretched and tied to two crosses. They were being crucified in the baking sun. Close by, Krails lounged on motorcycles talking and laughing. The big Krail leader stood apart from the rest. He stared straight ahead, seemingly right at us.

"Can that man see us?" Commander Beecham pointed at the Krail leader.

"No, sir. Even if he had my eyesight, and the chances of that are roughly two hundred million to one, this glass is screened so no one can see in."

"Good, but regardless—remove the grid," Beecham instructed.

The view immediately returned to an empty wasteland.

"Well, it's good news that they're both still alive. Jerry will be happy."

"But they won't last much longer out there," I said.

Beecham nodded. "Exactly. The Krails want us to barter for their lives, but I've no idea what they could want to barter *for*." He stood thinking and then clicked his fingers. "Got it. Maybe it's the armored truck."

"What's in that vehicle, besides Jerry?" I asked.

"Authorization codes, bank accounts numbers, personnel lists."

"But the Krails are just rogue outlaws, complete barbarians, sir. Why would they care about those sorts of things?"

"I hate to break this to you, Duran, but the Krails are a sophisticated organization living outside the fringe. They are armed, intelligent, and dangerous. For years, we've been feeding the media stories about them being cave people. That's absolute garbage. We just needed to keep the public away from them."

It was true. In papers like the *Free Times*, the Krails were always described as being "a small band of criminal animals out to enrich themselves by any means possible." This included torturing and killing men, women, even children. No act was too horrific for them. I'd always believed that they deserved exactly what they got. And according to the news stories I had read, the government had been successful in eradicating most of the Krails.

Now I realized what I should have worked out a while ago—that this story was obviously a lie, and I'd fallen for it hook, line, and sinker. On the journey in, I had seen a large group of Krails, so there was no way just a few of them were left; there must be hundreds, even thousands. And on a practical level, the ambush I had witnessed was carried out with almost military precision. What's more, for a supposedly "unsophisticated bunch of murderers," they seemed to possess some pretty sophisticated technology and skills.

They'd just managed to hack into an extremely advanced computer and communications system, after all.

Commander Beecham watched as I tried to make sense of it all.

"So," Commander Beecham said, "surprised?"

"Yeah. I guess there ain't no tooth fairies, either, huh?"

Beecham, Anderson, and I discussed what to do next. First, we needed to find out exactly what the Krails wanted.

"We have to speak to them," Beecham said at last.

"Well, *I'm* not volunteering to go out," Anderson said quickly. Then, seeing the look of disdain on Commander Beecham's face, he tried to backtrack. "I mean it would be highly dangerous, sir…and an hon—."

I interrupted his babbling. "Anderson's right, sir. All we might be doing is giving the Krails more hostages."

Commander Beecham thought about this. "Yep, that's definitely a possibility. But what choice do we have?"

Outside, the air was still, and the sun was now high in the sky. I was used to temperatures in the low hundreds but couldn't remember when I had felt so unbearably hot. As I fought for breath, sweat poured down my face and out of every pore on my body. Unnervingly, Commander Beecham seemed unaffected by heat. He looked cool, calm, and collected.

When Beecham and I reached the main entrance, we waited for a glider ball to exit ahead of us before we slid through the partially opened gates. As we stepped into the wasteland, the gates closed behind us. Except for the glider ball, we were alone and defenseless. I stared ahead. Through the shimmering heat, I could see the army of Krails and the two crosses.

Beecham stopped, raised his arm, and spoke into a tiny monitor on his watch.

"Anderson, take it out."

Anderson's face appeared on the screen. "Right, sir," he said.

The glider ball floated into the wasteland, but after traveling about fifty yards came to a halt, hovering above the ground.

Beecham spoke into the watch screen again. "Is that it?"

Anderson nodded. "Sorry, sir. These gliders aren't designed for use outside the compound. That's about the ball's limit."

"Then we'll just have to wait." Beecham leaned across to me and whispered, "Let's hope your idea works."

I'd come up with the plan in the observation room. It seemed a pretty good strategy. Commander Beecham and I would leave the fortress to barter with the Krails. Anderson would remain in the observation tower working the gates and the glider ball.

I had suggested using a glider ball to communicate to try and avoid the chance of either of us being taken hostage. If the ball could fly halfway to the Krails, they would have to come to us to barter. This would allow Beecham and I time to escape to the base in case of trouble. As I had explained it: "Art of War. During any negotiations make certain that your opponent is forced to meet you more than halfway."

As we waited, a cloud of dust and noise headed toward us. It was the leader Krail. His bike tore across the wasteland at high speed, heading for the glider ball. He pulled to a halt in front of it, got off his bike slowly, and stared at Beecham's face on the ball's screen.

"What's your name and what do you want?" Beecham asked.

"I'm Hunter, and we will give you your two men in exchange for one Krail and half a million cash."

Beecham laughed. "Well, for a start, we don't keep that kind of money on the base."

"You do. That's exactly the amount in General Stoker's safe, which you have the code for."

"Is he right?" I whispered.

The commander ignored me. "Okay, maybe we could do something like that."

"There's no maybe about it. If you want to do this, you'll get the cash. Now, have we got a deal?"

Beecham looked across at me. "We don't have any Krails, do we?" he asked quietly.

"There is one, the man Ruby and I captured, remember? The one we brought in on the armored truck."

Beecham turned. "You mean the prisoner?"

"Yes," the big Krail said, "and he has a name. We call him The Sandman."

"Whatever," Beecham said. "But that would be in complete violation of—"

"Then it's settled. We'll cook your men and feed them to the dogs." The Krail climbed back onto his bike.

One second passed. Then two. Then:

"Wait!" Beecham shouted.

Hunter glanced back at the glide ball screen. "So we *are* trading?"

Beecham hesitated. The staring match lasted a full half-minute. The commander was the first to break. "Okay. We'll do the exchange. One hour."

Hunter shook his head. "Half an hour." He motioned into the distance at the two crosses. "For their sakes."

Kicking his bike into gear, the big man rode off.

Before we could go to collect the Krail, The Sandman, from the detention unit, we used up a precious ten minutes of our allocated thirty minutes waiting for Beecham to return. He had insisted on going to retrieve the cash from General Stoker's safe alone.

Meanwhile, the remaining NSC officers began assembling by the main entrance. I had hoped there would be at least a few dozen. In fact, just thirteen remained, including Beecham and me—thirteen people who had to look, in the commander's words, "like a thousand."

When Beecham finally returned, he was carrying a large messenger bag I assumed held the money. He told me Anderson had just informed him that Krail reinforcements had arrived and at least three hundred were now assembled around the two crosses—not the news I wanted to hear.

It only took Beecham and me a few minutes to reach the detention unit. The commander used his thumbprint to open the solid steel entrance door. We marched down a long corridor until we reached a second door. It unlocked on our arrival. Inside, three NSC guards waited. They saluted as we appeared.

"At ease," Beecham ordered.

"Yes, sir," the guards chorused.

"We've come for the Krail prisoner—The Sandman."

"Yes, sir," said the fattest officer. "He's in jail house three, sir."

"Right, you—"

"Newton, sir, and this is Clydesdale and O'Henry." The fat officer pointed to a tall, muscled officer and a callow-faced youth.

"Well, Newton, you lead the way. Clydesdale, O'Henry, I want you up at the gates with the other officers."

The two guards headed out, and Newton accompanied us down another long passageway.

"Has he been any trouble?" Beecham asked.

"No, sir. Quiet as a lamb." Newton stopped in front of a barred cell containing a narrow single bed, a toilet, and a dirty sink. The Sandman sat in the center of the unit rocking back and forth. Newton unlocked the door.

"Stand up, prisoner," Newton ordered.

The Sandman ignored him.

"On your feet!" Newton bellowed. Still getting no response, he marched into the cell and tried to pull the Krail up. The Sandman screamed and kicked him in the kneecap, buckling his legs and dropping him to the floor. Then The Sandman wrapped his powerful legs around Newton's neck and started to crush the air out of him

I ran in and kicked the Krail in the head before twisting my arms around his neck in a submission hold. After a tense moment, The Sandman relaxed his hold and released a coughing and spluttering Newton.

Commander Beecham pulled out his gun and aimed it at The Sandman. "Newton and Duran, get that piece of Krail shit out of here."

CHAPTER ELEVEN

OFFICER NEWTON COVERED THE SANDMAN with his gun as we all marched back to the fortress entrance. On our way, a glider ball hovered into view and headed for Beecham.

"Yes?" the commander said on seeing Anderson's face on the ball's screen.

"Updating you again, sir. General Stoker and the NSC officer are still strapped to the crosses, but have been taken to a point about one hundred yards in front of the main entrance. And there are now over four hundred Krails outside the base. All are armed to the teeth."

"How do the general and the officer look?" I asked.

"Not good," Anderson replied.

"Thanks," Beecham said as we reached the compound entrance where the assembled NSC officers were waiting. They were all armed and looked ready to fight.

The commander ordered everyone to gather around. He was about to speak when Ruby walked into view.

Beecham stared at her. "What are you doing here?"

"Rodriguez has everything in hand. I thought I would be more useful here, sir."

"Mason, if I order you to do something, you do it. Understand?"

Ruby reddened. "Yes, sir."

"But in this instance, you've used your initiative. The more personnel we have here the better. You can stay."

"Thank you, sir," Ruby said quietly.

"Okay, everyone." Commander Beecham turned to address the crowd. "The enemy has asked to trade the Krail prisoner for the two NSC officers. I'm told there are several hundred of them out there—clearly they have numbers, but that doesn't matter. We have the firepower, we have the training, *we have the will to win.* So, everyone ready to go?"

"Yes, sir!" the officers said in chorus and started to chant: "NSC! NSC!"

Commander Beecham raised his hand, and the chanting instantly stopped. "Let's be clear. Whatever happens, we cannot let the Krails into the compound."

There were nods and shouts of agreement as Beecham spoke to the gliding ball hovering close by.

"Anderson, open the gates. Mason, Duran, you come with me."

The officers took up their positions guarding the entrance as the gates opened to let us out. Beecham pushed The Sandman forward, and together we marched on.

Ahead, Krails cut Jake and General Stoker down from their crosses. The men fell onto the dusty ground. Hunter yanked Jake up and pushed him forward. Another Krail grabbed General Stoker by the shoulder and lifted him as well.

Once Jake and the general were on their feet, Hunter and the other big Krail walked toward us with them.

Beecham called out when they were about twenty yards away. "Let our men go. We'll let your man go too and give you the money."

"Show me the cash," Hunter commanded.

Beecham lifted the messenger bag high into the air and opened it to reveal that it was filled with packages of bills.

"Sandman, check it," Hunter shouted.

The Sandman reached across and pulled out a bundle of notes, flicking through them with his fingers. Then he took out a single hundred-dollar bill and held it up to the light.

"Looks good to me," he said.

Beecham snatched the bill back from him, returned it to the bag, and slammed the bag shut.

Hunter smiled. "Okay. So you, the money, and The Sandman come to me. And Wreckage"—he indicated the large Krail who stood behind Jake—"bring that one over."

"No," Beecham said, emphatically. "That's not the deal. We agreed on both men."

"Okay, we'll just put them back up there then." Hunter pointed to the crosses. "Let them fry a little more."

Beecham stared at him but said nothing.

"Of course we could do this." Hunter pulled out a pistol and pointed it at General Stoker's head. "Then it would be one for one."

"What'll it be, NSC man? Haven't got a plan for this?" The Sandman asked, smirking.

"We need both. That was our agreement," Beecham said, ignoring the Krail.

Hunter sighed. "So, what are we going to do?" He stared into space before clicking his fingers. "I know. There is another way. How about this? I fight you. Hand-to-hand." He pointed at me. "If you win, you get both men and I get The Sandman and the cash. If I win, you get neither man, and I still get The Sandman and the money. Sound good?"

It was a stupid wager. Hunter was over six foot six and built like a pickup truck. He would tear me apart from the word "go."

I've been told that I have a reckless streak. I don't think that's true. I prefer to believe that I calculate the odds and then make a decision. I should have done that here, but I didn't. We had no choice. If we wanted to save General Stoker, I *had* to fight Hunter.

And I *had* to win.

"Commander, I can do this," I said.

Beecham thought for a few moments before nodding. He knew he had no option.

"You're on," I said to Hunter.

While Commander Beecham and the NSC officers stayed to guard The Sandman, Krail guards moved Jake and General Stoker some eighty yards back. Here the bikes were arranged in a large circle.

Beecham had delegated Ruby to be my second, and together, we stood in the circle and waited as a pickup truck charged towards us. Skidding to a halt, its two Krail occupants—Wreckage and another heavily tattooed Krail—leapt out and moved to either side of the tailgate. Slipping the bolts, they opened the back and quickly unloaded piles of dead branches and leaves. Other Krails grabbed the material and deposited it in a second smaller circle inside the line of bikes.

Ruby shook her head. "We've been conned," she whispered. "They suckered you into a fight that they were ready for and knew they would win."

"Ready, Boss," the Krail called Wreckage said.

Hunter stepped over the debris into the center of the smaller circle. "Come here," he said to me.

I stepped into the small circle, and as Hunter and I faced off, Wreckage picked up a large can of gasoline. He quickly poured this onto the wood and leaves. Then the Krail produced a silver antique lighter and flicked it open. He spun the lighter wheel and an orange and blue flickering flame shot up. Wreckage placed the lighter next to a branch. The gasoline on the wood caught fire instantly.

The Krail ran around the circle with the flaming branch, holding it over the wood and leaves, igniting them as he went. In moments, the circle was alight. A sheet of yellow flame leapt high into the sky.

Wreckage jumped through the flames and held a red bandana aloft.

Hunter stared at me. "Ready?" he asked. I nodded.

"The man remaining in the flaming circle wins," Hunter said.

The watching Krails pushed forward, chanting, "Krail! Krail! Krail!"

Hunter and I squared off. He moved toward me, dropping his guard. "Hit me," he said quietly.

Confused, I took a step back. Hunter moved forward again.

"Hit me," he repeated.

I had no idea why the Krail was asking this, but I didn't see why I shouldn't oblige him. I swung my fist, connecting with a solid right across Hunter's chin. The Krail's head tipped back, but his legs remained firm.

He shook himself and smiled at me. "Impressive," he said. "You hit like that in the outside world?"

I let my fists do the talking, releasing a barrage of blows to Hunter's ribs and chin. The big man dropped to one knee and spat blood. The watching Krails stopped chanting. They didn't need to worry. Hunter jumped cat-like to his feet and somehow got behind me. Taken off guard, I tried to turn but was too slow. Hunter's hands wrapped around my neck and began to squeeze.

The Krails chant started up again—louder now: "Krail! Krail! Krail."

Leaning close to me, Hunter whispered: "My real name is Gunner. Roy Gunner."

73

Was this a trick? It had to be.

I ignored the big man, and reaching back, grabbed him by the short hairs of his neck. Pulling with all my might, I slipped out of Hunter's grip. I moved away, waiting for the Krail's next move. I didn't have to wait long. He lashed out with his right leg, smashing me in the ribs and following up with a second kick high to my face. The force of the blow pushed me away. My legs crumpled, and I fell, my head just inches from the circle's dancing flames.

Ruby moved to help, but Krails grabbed her arms as their chanting reached a crescendo. "Krail! Krail! Krail!"

Hunter jumped forward onto me. He twisted my face around and started to grind it into the dirt. "I used to be NSC." Hunter leaned in close. But before he could continue, I slammed the back of my head into the side of his face. The big Krail reached up in pain. I rolled out from under him, put an elbow to his sternum, and pulled back his head by his hair.

Hunter ignored the pain. "For Christ's sake, *listen*," he said. "Everything they told you is a lie. Everything."

Would he ever shut up? I decided I would have to make him. I drove my forehead into his nose. The Krail shook his head, spat blood, and grinned.

"No drought, no famine, no war," he continued.

I released my grip slightly, confused. It was the opening he needed. The Krail reached down behind his back and pulled a dagger out. He pushed the weapon up to my throat and bent close. "Save us. Save us all," he whispered, and then suddenly eased his hold on the knife.

My hands came up, and I twisted the weapon away while simultaneously kicking up hard into Hunter's stomach. Using all my strength and straightening my legs, I levered the Krail up and pushed him forward. Hunter fell backward through the flames and out of the circle.

I had won.

So why did I feel like I'd lost?

The Krails went silent, exchanging inscrutable looks as Hunter lay in the dirt just beyond the circle of flame. Then Wreckage called out, "Kill them! Kill them all!"

"No!" Hunter commanded, leaping to his feet. "I gave my word."

The Krails stopped chanting. Hunter pointed to Ruby. "Let her go. I lost. He won fair and square."

I jumped over the flames to join Ruby.

"Let the prisoners go too." Hunter pointed to Jake and Stoker. Reluctantly, Krail guards released the men, and we all started to walk toward the base.

Seeing this, Commander Beecham handed The Sandman the messenger bag. "Go!"

The Sandman walked back. Reaching Jake and Stoker, he winked and spat at Jake's feet. "Good luck," he said.

"You too," Jake said, and head-butted him. I moved forward quickly and grabbed Jake, pulling him away.

"Leave him alone, you idiot." I looked back nervously. The Krails were waiting for a signal from Hunter. They were itching to attack.

"You okay?" Hunter shouted.

"Sure. He fights like a weakling," the Sandman said as he walked on.

Hunter raised his arm. "Easy," he said to the Krails.

As The Sandman reached the Krails, he dropped the satchel and grabbed a knife from one of them. He raised the weapon and threw it.

"Watch out!" Hunter yelled.

I turned, saw the dagger heading for Jake and pushed him away. The knife soared past us and hit Stoker, embedding itself in his back. The general screamed in agony and fell to the ground.

The NSC officers at the gate immediately started firing, cutting down The Sandman. The Krails responded—some fired guns while others shot volleys of arrows.

Ignoring the barrage of projectiles, Jake bent down to help Stoker.

I ran over and touched the general's neck and felt no pulse. He was dead. I tried to pull the general up anyway, looping his right arm around my back. Jake took the general's other arm. Together we lifted the dead soldier and ran back towards the base, while the NSC officers provided covering fire.

But the Krails weren't backing off. An arrow flew through the air and embedded in my thigh. I went down, dropping Stoker's body to the ground.

"Jake!" I shouted. "Help me."

He ignored me, continuing to drag the general's corpse the last few yards though the fortress gates. Meantime, the NSC officers had started to back up too, taking their dead and wounded comrades with them.

I struggled to stand and reached down to the arrow. "Leave it," someone shouted. I looked up to see Ruby running toward me through the hail of bullets and arrows.

Ruby tore material from her blouse, wadded it up, and stuffed it into my mouth. "Now, bite down," she ordered.

With a sudden effort, she snapped the arrow shaft off at its entry point. The cloth in my teeth barely muffled my scream of pain. Ruby helped me up and we headed for the steel main gates, which were almost closed. We just managed to squeeze through before the doors clanged shut.

Inside, Commander Beecham checked the condition of the remaining men. Of the nine officers still alive, two were wounded. Jake placed Stoker's body down next to the dead men. He looked up as I limped across.

"I'm going to tear your heart out, Teerman," I growled. "You left me out there to die."

"I had to decide between saving you and an NSC general. Easy choice." Jake looked across at Beecham. "And I could have him arrested for that comment, right, Commander?"

"Cool it, Teerman. Ruby, how are the systems holding up?"

Ruby pulled out the tiny computer tablet she had used earlier in the mainframe room.

"We've got around ninety minutes before they're able to enter the system again, and this time, I won't be able to stop them."

I knew once the hackers got in they would open the main gates. It would be us few against all of them. It'd be a massacre.

"You sure you can't slow them down anymore?" I asked.

"There is one possible way."

"What is it, Mason?" Beecham demanded.

"Commander." She motioned that they should move a distance away from the others. Jake followed. Together all three retreated to the edge of the main fortress building. Dragging my injured leg, I set out after them.

We grouped around as Ruby outlined her plan in simple, non-technical language. She could send a virus to infect the Krails' system. This would knock it out completely.

Commander Beecham smiled. "That's good," he said.

Yeah, too good. If it was really that simple, Ruby would have suggested it in the first place. But Beecham obviously didn't see any problems. "Go ahead. Do it."

Ruby didn't move. "That's the good news."

Beecham's smile disappeared. "What's the bad news?"

Ruby explained that the virus could also infect the NSC system and shut it down completely. We would lose control of everything, including the main gates. So it could be better to release the virus in isolated parts of the system like operations. But then we would run a greater risk of self-infection without contaminating the Krails' system.

Beecham stared at her. What Ruby was saying was the equivalent of taking a medicine that could kill you but could also possibly keep you alive.

It wasn't much of a choice.

I raised my hand. "I have a suggestion."

"Speak, Duran."

"Sir, may I remind you that Duran is only a candidate, and a failed candidate at that," Jake said.

Beecham stared at Jake. "You know what I think, Teerman? I think you read as a coward, a *selfish* coward. So far, Duran here has been stepping up to the plate. I'm ready to listen to anything he says. Duran, tell us your plan."

Jake visibly struggled to hide his anger as I outlined my strategy. I explained that we should accept the possibility of a total systems lockout and concentrate on stockpiling food, water, and weapons. We should also isolate an area we could secure so that we could fight off the Krails until help arrived. We might still die, but at least we would die honorably.

"Good strategy, Duran. Let's go with that," Commander Beecham said, and walked back to the officers.

"Listen up, we have a plan." He began to outline responsibilities. Jake would take three officers with him and go to the kitchen to stock up on food. Ruby would rejoin Rodriguez in the mainframe room and follow through on the effects of the virus. Beecham and I would clean out the arsenal. The rest of the men would gather up anything clean that could hold water and fill up the containers. We would need as much liquid as possible, enough to last for at least one to two days.

CHAPTER
TWELVE

THE ARSENAL WAS A HUGE, florescent-lit storage room with rows of metal shelving reaching up to the ceiling. Different types of weapons were stored on each shelf—guns, knives, explosives, and ammunition. Commander Beecham and I started loading the armaments onto a floating steel utility cart whose metal base was surrounded by six-foot high wire walls, covered by metal mesh roofing. Its tailgate had been lowered to allow access.

We chose cargo carefully, trying to source a range of weaponry and ammunition. We carried out our work swiftly and in silence, only too aware that time was ticking by.

As I searched through the high-tech guns and missile launchers, I discovered an old, ornate medieval crossbow. It had a beautiful oak base and an arched steel bow. Despite the urgency of our task, I couldn't resist bringing it down to take a closer look.

Beecham walked across to me. "I got that from a Krail prisoner a few months ago."

I stared at the weapon. I knew weapons like this. "This is from the eighteenth century," I said. "Made in the Ukraine, I think."

"You think?" he said, impressed.

"Yeah." I pointed to the elegant carving in the wood base and the beaten metal bow. Those were the clues to when and where it was made. "Actually," I said, "I once wrote a college paper on eighteenth-century weaponry."

"Which college?"

I thought about that. I could see the campus—the lush green grass lawns with modern buildings dotted around. The dorms were to the left of the main building, close by the cafeteria. A big three-story high glass fronted library sat adjacent to this.

"Hudson University. I collected old weapons, too, when I was taking my National Service, and then when I was in the force. It was a hobby."

"But you don't have any now?" Beecham asked.

I shook my head. They all had to go when I left the police.

Beecham reached up to a shelf and pulled down a quiver of arrows housed in a brown leather bag. They obviously were meant to be paired with the crossbow. The commander slipped the bag's strap over my shoulder.

"Perfect," he said. "You should keep them both."

I shook my head. "Sir! They're far too valuable."

"You take them. The bow will only collect dust here, and anyway, the NSC owes you for what you've done so far. I realize that technically once you are bounced from the candidate program you are out, but I'm going to see what I can do. Maybe I'll get them to consider taking you on or get you another shot at the candidacy." Beecham held out his hand. "Whatever happens, though, you're NSC in my book."

I didn't know what to say, so I just stammered out my thanks—then grimaced as I felt a pain shoot through my leg.

"Duran, you have to go to the infirmary. Clean that leg wound up and dress it properly," Beecham said.

I shook my head. "We don't have time for that. You need me here—what if we're attacked again?"

"You'll go to the infirmary, and that's an order, Duran. I can finish work here in the arsenal, but you've got to get back to fighting shape ASAP. You're no good to us injured."

Then he lifted his arm and spoke into his wristwatch. "Beecham to mainframe."

"Mainframe. Mason here," Ruby replied.

"Mason, how are your nursing skills?"

"I got some basic training when I was in the army."

"Excellent. Duran needs his leg dressed. Meet him down in the infirmary on level six."

"On my way."

79

The small infirmary looked brand new. Stainless steel cabinets lined the walls. Medical instruments were laid out on the slabs above the cabinets. Two large bulbous lights lit a sloping leather examination couch. Everything was spotlessly clean.

I swung around onto the divan, placed the crossbow and arrows on a shelf next to me, and stretched my legs out. The door slid open and Ruby entered. Glancing around, she whistled softly. "Impressive."

I nodded but said nothing. I was feeling tense.

"Don't like hospitals much?" Ruby asked, seeing my face.

"Not much."

"I hope you're not going to be a crybaby."

"I'll try my best."

Ruby unwound the temporary bandage, carefully feeling around the wound and touched the end of the arrowhead that was still embedded in my leg.

The laceration was festering. If it wasn't treated, it would get worse, and fast.

Ruby picked up a set of forceps on the cabinet top. Then she opened a wall-mounted cupboard and looked inside. It was packed full of bottles, tubes, and cartons of medicines. She grabbed a small plastic container and held it up. "Alcohol. Good."

Bending down, Ruby searched through a drawer. "Perfect." She took out a roll of bandages and some surgical tape.

"You obviously learned way more about medicine than I did when I was in the army."

"Let's hope I can remember everything I used to know." She placed the forceps, bandages, surgical tape, and bottle on the exam table stand. "Can you see any scissors?"

I pointed to a metal shelf to the right of the exam table. "There. I'll get them." I leaned across and handed the scissors to Ruby. She put them beside the bandages. Then, grabbing the forceps, Ruby told me to straighten my leg as much as I could.

"I could tell you that this won't hurt, but I won't," she said. "It's going to hurt like a bitch."

Lining up the forceps over the wound, she pressed down and yanked the arrowhead out of my leg. I stifled a scream.

"Yeah, I know, but the worst is over," Ruby said, holding up the forceps. They were gripping a metal arrowhead.

"That was *in* me?"

Ruby nodded, put the forceps down, and picked up the bottle. She opened it and soaked the laceration with the alcohol. I grimaced again as agony swarmed in the wound. This was almost as bad as getting shot.

"Now we just need to dress it." Ruby cut off a piece of surgical tape and used it to cover the wound. She wrapped several lengths of bandage around my leg, tying it up with more surgical tape.

Ruby stood back to admire her work. "How does that feel?"

I tentatively flexed my leg, swung myself off the couch, and then cautiously placed first one foot and then another on the tiled floor. Putting my full weight down, I tested the bandaged leg.

"Feels good," I said.

"You might need to have the muscle grafted together. But in the meantime, be careful just how much weight you put on the leg. Maybe head to the kitchen to see if they have anything to ice it down with."

I picked up the crossbow and arrows and smiled. "Thanks."

"No problem." Ruby walked with me to the door.

The door slid open and we entered a narrow steel-walled corridor.

"Where are you going now?" I asked.

"Back to the mainframe. I need to prep the virus. The kitchen for the ice is that way too. I saw it coming over here."

We saw Commander Beecham as we rounded the corner. He and three NSC officers were gently placing small transparent gel buttons on the steel floor.

"Duran, give me a hand here," Beecham said. "Mason, you can go through. These aren't armed yet."

Ruby hesitated. "What are they?"

"Electro-mines," Beecham explained. "Small, but incredibly deadly. The mainframe room's going to be our fallback position, so we're going to mine all the corridors that lead to it. Once you get inside, you'll have to stay put—or, boom!"

"Okay, I'll be off then, but don't forget to go the kitchen for ice, Hogan," she said, walking away.

Beecham watched me following Ruby with my eyes. "Come on, focus," he ordered, handing me a couple of the gel buttons and telling me to place them farther down the corridor.

I walked on, bent down, and carefully rested the buttons on the floor. Standing up, I went back to Beecham who took a remote control out of his pocket. "Once placed, these buttons are completely undetectable to the eye. They are top secret, brand-new out of NSC development... Stand back." He pointed the remote at the floor and pressed it. The light on the buttons changed from red to green. Now they were all armed.

A glider ball appeared from around the corner, hovering above the floor. Beecham moved his arm down and indicated to the glider ball to lower itself. As the ball flew close to the floor there was an explosion. It crashed—a fist-sized hole blown up through its center.

Beecham disarmed the buttons after his demonstration. They wouldn't be re-armed until everyone was assembled in the mainframe room. My leg had started to throb again, so I was happy Beecham allowed me to go down to the kitchen to find ice. The commander also asked me to tell Jake Teerman and the other officers assigned with him to hurry up and bring the food back to the mainframe room.

It took me about ten minutes to find the kitchen. I saw a large floating utility cart piled high with supplies next to the cold storage unit but no sign of Jake or the others.

I walked the length of the room. Like everything in the base, no expense seemed to have been spared designing and equipping the ultra-modern space. I'd wager that even in the wealthy zones, most kitchens were less than a tenth the size of this place and almost certainly couldn't afford the twelve-burner gas cookers, massive fridges, and the other equipment on show.

I opened one of the cabinet freezers and pulled out a big bag of ice. I pressed the bag to my injured leg; the relief was instantaneous and pleasure washed over me in a wave. Then I carried the bag over to the cart and dropped it on top.

Where was everyone?

I walked over to the giant refrigerator unit at the back of the kitchen. Maybe they were inside?

Grasping the large metal handle, I pulled. In the fortress's world of automatic doorways, it was refreshing to physically *open* a door. The heavy metal entrance swung back smoothly, and a blast of cold air hit me in the face. The storage unit lights flicked on, and through the icy haze I could see row after row of animal carcasses hanging from hooks. I couldn't remember the last time I'd seen a domestic farm animal, yet they must exist somewhere because these were the bodies of cows and pigs.

I shouted from the doorway: "Hello, anyone there?" Silence. I tried again. "Hello. Teerman?"

I took a step inside. What was that at the end—underneath one of the hanging slabs of meat?

Shivering, I reached what I'd seen. It was someone's hand! Bending down, I saw it was attached to a body. I peered at the corpse. It was an NSC officer—and his skull had been smashed in.

Further down, under the animal carcasses, I saw two more bodies. They were the other NSC officers who had been assigned to collect the food. Both appeared to have been murdered—hit hard over the head. The cadavers had started to freeze, but rigor mortis had not yet set in. These men had died within the hour.

I walked out quickly, stopped, and swung my crossbow around. I took the bow off, put my foot in the stirrup, and reached down to pull the wire back manually to cock it. Placing the bow carefully on my shoulder again, I pushed it behind my back. Taking one last check of the quiver of arrows that hung from my belt, I slammed the door closed.

I'd tend to the bodies later. I had to find their killer first.

CHAPTER THIRTEEN

Jake Teerman was dragging General Stoker's body over to the armored truck when I appeared.

"Teerman, I thought you were supposed to be working in the kitchen."

"I left that to the others, but you're just in time."

"For what?"

"To release Stoker's boy Jerry from the truck."

"You know who he is?"

"Sure, the general told me," Jake said. "We can't just leave him in there." He reached down for Stoker. "Help me with him, will you?"

"Why?"

"You'll see. Just lift him upright."

I helped hoist Stoker's body up in front of the armored truck's backdoor. Holding the body with one hand, Jake used his other to hit the intercom.

"Jerry," he said.

"Who's that?" a voice asked over the intercom.

"Jake Teerman, Jerry. I'm an NSC officer. I'm gonna try and get you out of there."

"How you're going to do that? Is my dad out there? Is he alive?"

"As a matter of fact, he is," Jake said.

I looked over at him and mouthed the word, "What?"

"Dad! Dad!" Jerry shouted.

"He's resting at the moment, Jerry, but he suggested a way to get you out."

"That's just like my father," Jerry said, sounding happy. "What do you have to do?"

"Don't worry about that." Jake put his finger to his mouth. He whispered for me to take the general's entire body weight as he forced open Stoker's eyes.

"We just have to get these eyes onto the I-Lock, Duran."

I pushed General Stoker's body forward and Jake lined up the man's eyes, placing them open, inside the sockets of the I-Lock.

"Now bring his hand up and put his thumb into that indentation," Jake said quietly.

I raised the dead general's hand and did as Jake asked.

"Ready when you are, Jerry," Jake said.

A green light popped on next to the intercom and sturdy locks could be heard unbolting from inside the vehicle. After a few moments the heavy metal door swung open and a thin, geeky man in his early twenties appeared.

Jerry took a deep breath as he looked around. "Ah, fresh air—" Red blood spurted from a hole in his chest, just below his collarbone, and he dropped dead next to his father's body.

"Jake!" I shouted. 'You killed him. You've killed the general's son!"

"Sure did," Jake said, but before he could turn the gun on me I aimed the crossbow right at his heart.

"You killed the men in the kitchen too," I said, my hand shaking.

Jake shrugged. "Collateral damage. They weren't keen on me coming out here."

He smiled. "Duran, do you have any idea what's in that truck?"

"Besides Jerry?"

"Yeah. I still can't believe you thought I'd risk so much just to let him out—even if he is the general's kid."

"So why did you do it?"

"For the *diamonds*. Huge stones the size of your fist. Billions of dollars' worth. Stoker told me all about it while we were out in the wasteland. I made a deal with the Krail leader, Hunter. He said he'd give me safe passage in exchange for half the diamonds. Screw the NSC, Duran. I'll be rich beyond our wildest dreams. You can be, too—just put the crossbow down."

I laughed, annoying Jake. "What the hell's so funny?" he asked.

"You. Only you'd believe that stupid story. You've killed Jerry and all those men for nothing. There isn't anything in that truck except files and computer readouts."

"Stoker told me—"

"And you fell for it," I interrupted. "I guess he likes to watch the newcomers drool."

"No, no, that can't be right."

"Go check, then. I'll wait."

Jake stared at me, then he stepped back onto the armored truck, still keeping his gun up and trained on me. Inside, large, flat, black metal containers were spread across the floor. A thick blue tape with the words *Property of the NSC* ran lengthwise over each of the lids, providing a seal.

Jake moved the pistol to his left hand. With his right hand, he pulled out a knife tucked into his waistband.

I took a step forward and stared in through the truck door, my crossbow still in hand.

"I told you, no diamonds."

"Oh, yeah?" Jake quickly cut a seal with his knife and levered the lid off the nearest container. The open box revealed a dazzling array of gemstones that shimmered—even in the low light in the interior of the truck.

Jake laughed. "See, Duran?"

I frowned. "You were right," I said. "There's a fortune in there. Spend it wisely." And I slammed the truck door shut.

Jake fired, but the bolts of the heavy door automatically locked in place and his bullets pinged off the steel interior and dropped harmlessly to the floor.

I couldn't just leave the general and his son's bodies baking in the hot sun. I pulled Jerry up, linked my arms under his armpits and dragged him along, his feet trailing on the ground. I know this wasn't very respectful, but it was the only way I could move him on my own.

It took me about five minutes to reach the kitchen and the cold storage unit. Dragging Jerry, I walked past the animal carcasses and reached the officers' bodies sprawled on the floor. I lowered Jerry next to them and leaned heavily against the wall to get my breath back. Then I went out again to collect the general's body and bring it back.

I figured that if someone died on the base, they would usually be put in a casket and transported to the city for burial. But I had no idea where to find caskets, and anyway, getting the bodies out of the fortress was impossible at the moment. So I decided to leave Jerry, the general, and the others in the freezer.

I'm not a religious guy. Too much bad had happened in the world recently for me to believe anymore in a compassionate deity. But I knew that maybe some of these dead men had held a faith. I had been bought up a Catholic and decided to recite a prayer I had learned as a child.

Self-consciously, I began aloud:

> "God our Father,
> Your power brings us to birth,
> Your providence guides our lives,
> and by Your command we return to dust."

I stopped as I tried to remember how the rest of the prayer went. Then:

> "Lord, those who die still live in Your presence,
> their lives change but do not end.
> I pray in hope for my family,
> relatives and friends,
> and for all the dead known to You alone.
>
> In company with Christ,
> Who died and now lives,
> may they rejoice in Your kingdom,
> where all our tears are wiped away.
> Unite us together again in one family,
> to sing Your praise forever and ever."

I crossed myself, turned, and headed for the exit. Closing the freezer door, I walked over to the floating cart. It was loaded with enough catering supplies to last for at least four days—though if the Krails broke into the base, we wouldn't make it alive for long enough to eat it.

I grasped the cart's handle, put slight pressure on it, and moved the cargo forward.

Guiding the floating transporter through the maze of narrow corridors, I finally arrived back at the mainframe room. The officers gathered inside were elated to see the food I brought, but their expressions quickly transformed from joy to horror once they saw the blood soaked into my coveralls.

Then I had to tell them about Jake Teerman, and the deaths of Jerry and the other officers.

I tried to go gently, but the longer I talked, the worse the mood inside the mainframe got. Commander Beecham seemed particularly affected by the news. "I watched Jerry grow up," he muttered, the color draining from his face. "The general, and now him—they've really taken everything from me."

"You okay, sir?" Ruby asked.

Beecham raised his hand and the room quieted. A moment passed. Then: "Sorry. Yes. I just lost it there for a second."

"Pretty understandable, sir," I said. "Under the circumstances."

"It's not just Jerry and the general, you know. I'm starting to worry about my judgment. I supported Stoker's decision about awarding that candidate the position. Teerman seemed to have everything we were looking for in an NSC officer. We were obviously both completely wrong. Anyone but him would have been a better choice."

I said nothing. Instead, I pointed at the schematics of the base spread out on a table in front of me.

"Where are we on defense, sir?" I asked the commander.

Beecham explained that while I was away he had ordered Anderson to remain in the observation tower and supply regular updates. And six other officers had been sent to guard the front entrance.

Beecham pointed at the overhead monitors, which showed the officers moving into position. "Only way in or out," Beecham said. "They are stationed just inside with enough firepower to hold the Krails off." He pointed to the schematics. "There are three corridors leading to the mainframe and I have laid button mines in each of them. Now that you're back, I'll arm them."

"What's the progress on the virus?" I asked Ruby and Rodriguez.

The women confirmed that they had held off the hackers up to now and prevented them from moving further into the main computer. They also had the virus ready to launch.

"But as I told you," Ruby said, "although this could destroy the Krails' computer system, it could also wipe out the mainframe computer system."

"Better destroyed than fall into Krail hands," Beecham said.

"That may be sooner than we thought." Rodriguez finished typing into her tablet. "Looks like they've almost broken through the operation's hard drive."

A glider ball hovered into view and stopped in front of Commander Beecham.

"They're on their way, sir," Anderson reported.

We looked up at the monitors. We could see Hunter leading a battalion of Krails over the crest of the hill onto the flat, dusty wasteland. Some were on foot. Others rode on bikes. Over the mainframe speakers we could hear their screams, shouts, and chants of "Krail! Krail! Krail!" The blood-curdling cries grew ever louder as the horde advanced.

On another monitor, I watched the officers guarding the main gates. They could hear the approaching Krail army and looked tense and nervous.

We continued to watch as Hunter and the Krail bikers arrived to join other Krails already camped just outside the main gates.

Hunter aimed his bike directly at the entrance and opened the throttle. He accelerated at high speed towards the entrance. Nearing the gates, Hunter reached into his leather jacket and produced a small metal ball. Then he jumped up, balanced on the bike's seat, and hurled the ball. It flew higher and higher, just managing to clear the top of the gates.

Hunter dropped down onto his bike and broke hard. His back wheel spun, kicking a plume of dust into the air. The vehicle halted inches from the entrance.

The officers inside fired at the ball as it fell. Bullets hit it but bounced off harmlessly. The ball slammed into the ground and opened up, throwing out a greenish gas that filled the area.

We watched in horror as the officers ran from gas. But the fumes spread rapidly, pursuing and enveloping the retreating soldiers. Some made futile attempts to cover their noses and mouths with their hands. But it was useless. The officers fell to the ground, choking, gasping, and vomiting. Within seconds, they were dead.

The ball started to suck the gas back inside itself. Simultaneously an enormous explosion rocked the entrance and a huge hole appeared in the gates. Hundreds of chanting, screaming Krails ran through it into the compound.

We stared in disbelief at the monitors.

"Sir." The voice came from the hovering glider ball.

"Yes, Anderson," Beecham said testily.

"I think Krails could be on their way up to me."

"Barricade the door, Anderson. You know that surrender is not an option," Beecham said.

"Yes, sir, but…. Oh God! I think I can hear them." He stopped. "They're outside. I can hear them. God, there's got to be hundreds!"

"The door should hold them, officer," Beecham said, reassuringly.

"Hopefully," Anderson said, and then frowned. "Oh no. I think—" The glider ball screen went blank. The sound of static filled the room.

The room went silent. We were all thinking it: Anderson was dead, and we could be, too, any second now.

I looked back up at the monitors. Hunter was walking toward the armored truck.

"Anyway he can open that?"

Beecham shook his head. "Impossible," he said confidently. But no one appeared to have told Hunter that. He stared at the I-Lock on the door of armored truck and raised his hand. On the monitor, I saw a curly-haired teenage Krail push through the crowd. He carried a small tablet.

"What do you think, Dice?" Hunter asked the young Krail.

Dice shrugged. "Easy." He walked up to the I-Lock and typed rapidly on the tablet. There was a click from the lock, but the door remained closed.

Hunter stared. "Lost your touch?"

Dice ignored his leader and returned to the tablet.

We held our breath and waited. After about twenty seconds of typing he stopped. "That should do it, Boss."

"Open it, then," Hunter said.

Dice brought his index finger hard down on the tablet. There were clicking sounds as bolts were unlocked. The truck door swung open. An angry Jake, gun in hand, tried to focus his eyes in the bright sunlight.

"All right, Duran," he said, "you've had your—" He stopped when he saw the Krails.

"Take him!" Hunter shouted.

Jake raised his weapon to fire but the Krails were too fast. Hands grabbed him and dragged him out of the truck.

CHAPTER FOURTEEN

"**S**HOULD I RELEASE THE VIRUS now, sir?" Ruby asked Beecham. The commander didn't answer. A line of sweat trickled down in front of his right ear, and he stood rigid, transfixed by the screens above us.

"Sir?" Ruby said. "Sir, we might not be able to save ourselves, but we can protect the NSC."

Still Beecham said nothing. Ruby and I exchanged worried glances.

A radio on Beecham's hip came to life and a crackly, distant male voice could be heard. "Base Camp Seventeen—" Static interrupted the voice.

Beecham grabbed the radio. "This is Commander Beecham, Base Camp Seventeen, come in."

There were a few moments of silence before the same voice, without the static, replied: "Base Camp Seventeen, this is NSC Recon Battalion Eighty-Three. Report."

"Good to hear you, Eighty-Three," said a visibly relieved Beecham, "Seventeen under heavy Krail attack. Base has been breached. Mainframe is secure currently but compromise imminent. Requesting assistance."

"Roger, Seventeen. We're about five miles north by northeast of Base Camp. Can you hold them off for a few more minutes?"

"Count on it," Beecham said. "Base Seventeen out."

The commander put the radio back and addressed us. "They won't breach those mine defenses, that much I do know," he said. "So we can hold them off until help arrives."

We continued to watch the monitors as Hunter and the Krails wound their way along the passageways to reach a corridor that led directly into the mainframe room. Hunter raised his hand to the Krails behind. "Stop!"

Hunter pointed at Jake. "Bring him."

Krails pulled Jake to their leader. He was quivering with fear.

"I had you pegged as a coward from the first moment I saw you." Hunter grasped Jake's arm. He pushed the man forward. "You want to run?"

Jake looked down the empty corridor. "Make it to the end of the corridor, and I'll let you live," Hunter said.

"Sure. I run and you shoot me, big man. That's not much of a choice," Jake said.

"I give you my word as a Krail," Hunter said. "And the others won't shoot you either." He raised his hand and shouted to the Krail army behind him. "Lower your weapons."

The Krails obeyed. Some put their armaments on the floor, while others pushed their guns back into their waistbands.

"Now make up your mind." Hunter pulled up his gun and pointed it directly at Jake. "Run or you're dead anyway."

Jake took a deep breath and released a roar. He started to sprint down the corridor. Moments later his left foot exploded as he stepped on a mine. Blood and bones shot out, plastering the steel corridor walls. His right foot hit another mine and exploded too, taking half his leg.

Screaming in agony, Jake dropped forward into a pool of his own insides. His arms exploded, then his left shoulder disintegrated as, piece by piece, the man's body was torn to shreds by the mines.

We could hear the thunder of the explosions through the steel door.

For a long second, nobody spoke. Then I piped up: "Sir, the mines."

"Yeah, I know, I know," Beecham snarled. He spoke rapidly into his radio: "Eighty-Three, this is Seventeen. ETA?"

"Three minutes," a voice instantly replied.

Outside we could see the Krails charging down the corridor past what remained of Jake's body. Moments later there was the sound of banging on the mainframe room door.

"Release the virus!" Beecham ordered.

Ruby reached for the tablet.

"No," I said, grasping her hand.

"Sir?" said Ruby, looking at Beecham.

"We don't have time to debate this, Duran," the commander said. "Let Mason do her work."

"They knew how to get by our defenses. They knew about the men behind the gates. They knew about Jake in the truck. They knew where we were and how to get here, and they knew about the mines. Have you asked yourself how?" I asked.

"Because the Krails aren't stupid, Hogan, how do you think?" Ruby said.

"Knowing *one* defense—okay, that could have been luck. Knowing two—maybe that's down to being prepared. But all the rest?" I looked over at Beecham. "You told me those button mines were in development at the NSC. Who knew about them?"

Beecham shrugged. "Just a few people."

"And the armored truck? They got in there in seconds, hacking through what should be a foolproof system."

"Obviously they must have had access to the security schematics," Beecham said, "which are…" He stopped.

"Which are stored in the mainframe," I said, finishing.

Why hadn't I realized earlier? The answer was simple—because *she didn't want me to see.* She'd played me. She'd played us all. In the shower, she had been the only woman who had covered her breasts. This was a woman who had admitted that she had worked as a stripper. What was she hiding?

"People, can we have this debate some other time!" Rodriguez shouted, pointing at the monitors. Chanting and cheering Krails hurled themselves against the buckling mainframe door. "They're getting through."

"We haven't got time for this," Ruby said.

I pulled my loaded crossbow up and pointed it directly at her.

"Take off your shirt."

"Duran," Rodriguez said, "what are you doing?"

"Ruby," I said. "Take off your shirt!"

"Duran, lay the crossbow down now. That's an order," Beecham said.

"She's a Krail, Commander. I can prove it."

"You're lying," said Ruby defiantly. "Commander, we're wasting time with this lunatic."

Holding the crossbow with one hand, I tried to snatch the tablet off her.

"Commander!" Ruby shouted.

Beecham looked from Ruby to me and then to the door, which was about to collapse.

He'd made a decision.

"Maybe you should do as Hogan said. Remove your shirt, Candidate Mason," Beecham ordered.

Ruby spun around, kicking Rodriguez in the head, and grabbing her gun. Using Rodriguez for cover, she fired rapidly twice, once at me as I ducked behind a control panel, the other at Beecham, hitting him in the stomach. The commander buckled, his abdomen already soaked in blood.

Rodriguez reached out to try and take back the gun, but she wasn't fast enough. Ruby fired twice at Rodriguez, point blank. The woman collapsed, bleeding on the tiled floor.

Ruby pulled off her shirt to reveal an eye-mark branded just above her left breast. I'd seen that mark before, in pictures in newspapers. Everyone knew what it meant.

The Eye—the Mark of the Krail!

"Death to the NSC. Long live the Krails!" Ruby fired at me as she began to type on the tablet screen.

"Stop! Don't do it!" I shouted.

Ruby went to shoot me again, but her gun clicked empty. I jumped from behind the control panel, my crossbow at the ready.

"You're not going to do that, Hogan." Ruby smiled.

My finger tightened on the bow's trigger, and then stopped. For a moment—just a split-second—Ruby's face was replaced with another woman's. The woman who shot Max.

Behind me, the mainframe door started to give.

"Forgive me." I pulled the crossbow trigger.

The arrow lanced through the air, heading towards Ruby. It stopped in mid-air, inches from her eyes.

There was a blast of white light.

I shook my head. *Where was I?* The mainframe room was gone. Now I was floating, facing a window, enclosed by a sheer white wall. I was in some sort of chamber. I looked down. I was naked. Outside I saw two white-coated men approach. They peered into the chamber. One man pulled at the entry, releasing it with a loud click.

As the door opened, my feet gently lowered onto the white-tiled chamber floor. The men caught me as I fell forward.

"Take this." One of the technicians handed me a blanket.

I tried to speak but I couldn't. I opened my mouth but nothing came out.

I wrapped the blanket around me as the men led me out of the chamber into a dazzling bright room. Here I slumped down into a metal chair.

In the far distance, I could see two figures approaching. I tried to focus my eyes, but the figures remained blurred, their footsteps reverberating, echoing inside my head. Something was wrong with my hearing. All I heard was a low murmur, like a droning engine.

After a few moments, I was able see clearly, but what I saw made me question my sanity. Commander Beecham and General Stoker were walking toward to me.

The general was the first to speak. "Congratulations, Duran," he said.

I tried to say something but could still only utter a croaking sound.

"Give it a minute," Stoker said. "Coming out of VR is disorientating."

"You've been at zero gravity for a considerable time. You have to adjust," Beecham added.

"What? What's happening?" I asked, my voice cracking.

"What's happening is that you've made it. You're NSC," said Stoker.

"But the Krails—"

"All part of the program. You've just been subjected to the most rigorous and advanced VR program ever devised," Stoker said.

"What?" My head swam. Pain pounded behind my eyes. "You're saying all that… it wasn't real?" I cried out, my rage rising.

I tried to stand and screwed up my fist. I didn't care what they'd do to me; I was going to hit one of these grinning idiots. Beecham grabbed my arm and easily pulled it back. My arms shook; my strength was gone, drained by hours—days?—in the chamber.

"Calm down, soldier. Take a deep breath," Beecham said.

I stared at them and smiled. "Of course. You're joking. You're just winding me up."

"We're telling the truth. It's a very sophisticated program, Duran, and though I understand your feelings, it's never a good idea to try and hit a superior officer," General Stoker said.

"You're serious?"

"Of course." Beecham smiled. "But if we'd told you before that from the moment you stepped onto the transporter in the station until just now you were going to enter a simulation, would you have believed us?"

"And more's the point, we couldn't tell you, anyway. It would invalidate the test. You do see that, don't you?" Stoker asked.

I stared at the two men. I still felt like beating the hell out of them. I tried to move forward, but I didn't have the strength.

"What you're experiencing is a perfectly natural reaction—your anger, your feelings of betrayal. But what we're telling you is good news, I promise," Stoker said.

I didn't answer but glanced back at the chamber I'd just come out of. It was just one of many that lined the back wall of the room. They all had matte white doors with single long windows cut into them.

I pointed at the containers. "Is there anyone else in the others?"

"Take a look," Stoker said.

I took a tentative step forward. My strength seemed to have finally returned to my legs.

With Beecham leading and Stoker by my side, I slowly made my way over to the chamber next to the one I had just come out of. I peered in through the window and saw a naked body floating in the chamber. It was Ruby, but the Krail marking was now missing from her breast.

"Ruby's alive?" I asked, bemused.

"Of course. She's simply in a state of suspended animation," Stoker said.

"You have to understand, Duran, that the NSC is the backbone of our society," Stoker told me. "It's the glue that keeps it together. So we have to be sure that whoever joins us is absolutely the right candidate. We have to push everyone who applies to their limits."

"So I was never in any real danger?" I asked as the two white-coated technicians returned, carrying a gurney between them. They walked past Ruby's chamber and stopped some ways down the line.

"Let me show you something, Duran," Stoker said.

Together we walked to the chamber the technicians had just entered. Looking in, I saw that the body of a candidate was being lifted from the ground and placed on the gurney.

"This one didn't make it," Stoker said.

"He's dead!"

"It has to be real," Stoker explained. "To make the test work. It's the only way. And everyone who signs up to take part is made fully aware that they could be injured or even die during the testing. In signing the contract form you agreed to that. You remember doing that, don't you?"

"Yes, but I didn't think …"

"Perhaps you should have."

He was right. We all should have.

"If you'd made one slip, one wrong move, you too would have been killed in the program," Commander Beecham said as he walked to join to us.

It was unbelievable. I didn't need to ask about the other candidates who were removed "injured" during the training. Despite the denials at the time, they were obviously dead, too.

"What about your son, Jerry? You allowed him to be killed?"

Stoker chuckled. "That wasn't my son—just a Krail that we'd reprogrammed to believe was my boy."

"We needed to record your empathetic reactions, you see. And boy, did you pass with flying colors!" Beecham said.

"Who are all those people in there?" I indicated the other chambers.

"Some are potential candidates, and some are ex-candidates that we use from time to time, but most are captured Krails," Stoker said.

"Like Hunter?"

"Yes. He was NSC once, and second in line for commanding officer. The Krails captured him and turned him somehow. But we caught him again, along with hundreds of other Krails."

"How many chambers are there exactly?"

"Hundreds," Beecham said.

"I know there's a lot to take in, Duran, but why don't you go with Commander Beecham, get something to eat, and he can answer all your questions."

As Beecham and I walked to the canteen, my head was still reeling with what I had been told. Part of me believed that I should just ask to leave and then reveal to the world what was happening out here. But maybe that was stupid! We were all desperate to join the NSC and prepared to take any risk, so perhaps none of us had anyone to blame but ourselves.

Entering the canteen, I saw it was exactly like the one in the VR world, which made sense. Why not just copy what was already in the real world?

The room was full of officers, but a reserved table had been set aside for me.

I sat down and a server immediately carried over a huge plate of steak and chips and a large glass of water, putting them down in front of me.

"Eat up. Only the best for you now," Beecham said.

He watched as I cut into the meat and shoved it into my mouth, taking a swig of water afterward. I was even hungrier and thirstier than I'd thought, and the food was beyond wonderful.

"Slow down." Beecham smiled. "No one's going to take it away."

I said nothing for the next few minutes and savored every mouthful. Finally, my stomach full, I sat back in my chair.

"Any more, Officer Duran?" Beecham asked.

I shook my head. "No, sir. Thank you, sir," I said. "I was really hungry, though."

"It's to be expected. In the VR world, the food you eat isn't real. Now, I'm sure there are lots of questions you want to ask."

"I've been thinking about Ruby Mason, sir."

Beecham smiled.

"No, not like that, sir. It's just, I thought I'd *killed* Ruby, shot her, and yet she was still alive in the chamber, right?"

"That's because in your program Ruby was just a symbiote."

"So she does exist or doesn't exist. Which is it, sir?"

"Let me explain. Every candidate's brain is individually mapped out, and then a program is set up to test their emotional responses: fears, loyalty, response to crises. All the information is fed into the mainframe and then the candidate's program begins. At the same time, some individuals are chosen to become part of other people's programs. These are symbiotes. So as a symbiote, Ruby was a traitor in your program. In her program, *you* are a symbiote—and a traitor too."

"Sir," a voice said behind me. Beecham turned to face a tall, thin NSC officer, who stood to attention and saluted.

"Duran, follow Officer Lestor here. He'll fit you up with your new uniform and then I'll give you a tour of the facility."

CHAPTER FIFTEEN

W EARING MY NEW BLUE AND white officer's uniform should have been a highlight for what had been an incredible day. But as I'd stood in front of the full-length mirror in the uniform room, I felt strangely empty. Officer Lestor seemed to notice. He hovered around nervously after the uniform was fitted, shifting his weight from one foot to the next as he watched me pretend to admire myself in the reflection.

"Is everything okay, sir?" Lestor asked as I continued to stare into the mirror.

"Yes, of course. The uniform fits perfectly."

It was true. The suit fit my body perfectly. But still…

"Looking good, Officer Duran." Beecham entered the fitting room. "Ready for your tour?"

"Yes, sir. Ready." I headed for the door.

"You may have noticed, Duran, that not everyone we're passing is an NSC officer," Beecham said as we walked away from the fitting room.

Actually, I hadn't. I'd been too preoccupied. This corridor was full of people, but only now did I notice that only some of them wore the blues and whites of an officer. Others were dressed in red-and-yellow uniforms or green-and-yellow jackets and trousers.

"These different uniforms reflect the fact that this complex, Base Camp Seventeen, has two purposes. One is training and recruitment—choosing and honing officers such as yourself—but the other is equally important," Beecham said.

I knew exactly what that was. "Diamond mining," I said.

"Why'd you say that?" Beecham asked, puzzled.

"I saw it in the program. Diamonds were being shipped in the armored truck."

Beecham shook his head. "Diamonds? No, it was supposed to be cash. Are you sure?"

"Absolutely. I saw the containers full of gems."

"There must have been a glitch. It's to be expected with such sophisticated technology. The system must have picked up on something in the real world." Beecham stopped in front of two huge steel doors. He placed his eye before an I-Lock, a light turned from red to green, and the doors slid open.

We stepped into a large elevator, which almost immediately started to descend, accelerating as it went. After about a minute, it slowed and finally came to a smooth halt. The doors opened, and Beecham motioned for me to exit.

"This was what the program picked up from the real world," he said.

I was in a dimly lit cavernous tunnel, which had other smaller tunnels running off it. Krails were tipping rocks into floating transporters. They were filthy and dressed in ripped shorts and shirts. The NSC personnel supervising them were dressed in blue waterproof coveralls and wore helmets with clear Perspex visors.

As I watched, a light on the front of the lead transporter glowed green. Most of the Krails saw this and moved away from the vehicle. Those that didn't were pulled back by NSC personnel.

The transporter started up and traveled at high speed towards us before veering to the right toward three large open elevators. The vehicle floated onto the first of these and seconds later the elevator descended.

"So, Duran," said Beecham as we walked further into the tunnel, "you were right about diamonds. That's what we're mining here. This particular tunnel is about a thousand feet below ground, and our NSC mining operatives are in charge of this part of the operation. They blast the rocks, and the Krails do the grunt work, breaking the stones up before collecting them and filling the transporter. The carts are taken down below where the rocks are crushed and x-rayed for diamonds. The gems are then separated."

"And where do these Krails live?"

"They are housed here too."

"Below ground?"

"Why not?"

A Klaxon wailed and red lights flashed in the tunnel. Beecham told me to move back as the NSC personnel herded the Krails to one side of the tunnel.

"Blasting," he said.

Moments later, a loud explosion sounded, and further along the tunnel, rocks cascaded from the wall. Krails ran back to load new rocks into baskets even before the dust had settled.

"We've had to dig deeper and deeper tunnels as the mining has continued," Beecham said as we walked on.

We reached another transporter. Pointing to the cart, Beecham explained that each load of rocks usually only produced one or two small diamonds. As he spoke, a short, thin Krail struggled to tip his basket filled with rocks into the vehicle. He tripped and fell on his face, and his load of rocks scattered across the stone floor.

I moved forward to help the man, but Beecham pulled me back. "Leave it, Duran. Not our call."

An NSC operative ran across and stood over the Krail. "Pick it up," he ordered, pointing to the basket. The Krail tried to stand, revealing a large bloody gash on his right leg. He bent down to grab the basket, lost his balance, and fell again. The NSC official pulled out a taser and shocked the Krail.

"Again!" he shouted.

The Krail was still reeling from being Tasered and barely had the strength to stand. Irritated, the officer twisted the dial to full power. He leaned forward and pushed the gun into the Krail's arm. The Krail shook violently and collapsed face-down.

"Here, you,"—the operative pointed at two Krails—"Dump him in the elevator."

The Krails picked up the body of their fallen comrade and carried him away.

Beecham turned to head back. "Come on, Duran."

Reluctantly I followed him. "Sir, was that man dead?"

"I don't know, but don't worry, there's lots more where he came from. We're pulling around half a million dollars' worth of diamonds out of the ground every twenty-four hours. That's enough to fund the entire NSC. The food, the housing…the perks."

I nodded. "Along with everything else I guess, right? The outreach programs, the soup kitchens."

"That's correct," said Beecham. "Oh, and here's something you may want to remember. Every mine we open, we open all the way down on Level Twenty-one. Now come on, Duran. I'll show you your new quarters. You'll be impressed."

As we made our way back, I couldn't get the image of the Krails in the mines out of my head. I tried to rationalize. Perhaps I was overreacting. The Krails were criminals. And there was no doubt that the NSC used a part of the money they got from the diamond revenue to fund their charity work. The same was true of the candidates who died. It was their decision, wasn't it? So didn't the ends justify the means?

"Duran, are you making a note of where we're going?" Beecham asked, breaking into my thoughts.

"Yes, sir. We went left out of the elevator, right, second left, and third right, and then down this corridor, past these doors all of which are equipped with I-Locks and which I'm guessing are quarters for my fellow officers."

"Impressive. But then that's why you were chosen." Beecham stopped in front of a door marked 316. "This one's yours. You'll have off-base housing, too, but when you're on duty you'll stay here."

He indicated the I-Lock. "Go ahead. It's already preprogrammed for your eyes."

I placed my eye on the I-Lock. The light next to the lock turned from red to green. As I moved back, the door slid open. The room was modern, bright, and clean. To the right was a duvet-covered king-size bed. A large, micro-thin TV hung from the opposite wall. Under it was an antique mid-twentieth century modern desk and chair. A tablet, laptop, and phone sat on top of it. A three-seater blue cloth sofa was positioned against the far wall. A small, fully-equipped kitchenette had been fitted into an enclave at the back.

"All the comforts of home," said Beecham. "You can see we've chosen a few artistic furnishings for you too. That's an Andy Warhol print of Marilyn Monroe—a famous actress back in the nineteen sixties. If you get bored around here, you can run a training program. It's available twenty-four seven. They're a lot of fun. They're in the room near the canteen."

Beecham walked to the door. Stopping, he turned around. "Report to my office six a.m. sharp tomorrow morning. We'll talk about your assignment then.

And one more thing." Beecham snapped to attention and saluted. "Welcome aboard," he said as the door slid closed behind him.

I walked over to the bed, sat on it, and laid back. It was very comfortable. I hadn't slept in a bed like this since… I hesitated. The fact was, I'd never slept in a bed like this at all.

I got up and walked to the kitchen. I opened the overhead storage cupboards and saw plates, cups, glasses, and pots and pans. All were in the blue and white colors of the NSC. A washer-dryer was next to the electric stove, and above this, a small sliding cutlery drawer.

I mentally ticked off the rest of the kitchen equipment. Garbage bin—check; sink—check; hot and cold running water—check. The water quota here was probably way higher than at my old apartment too. The only thing missing was a shower. Where was that? As if the room had read my mind, a white door at the end of the kitchen slid open to reveal a tile-lined room. Here I saw a beautifully designed space with a shower, toilet, sink, and bathroom cabinet.

I sat on the sofa. It was, of course, the most comfortable sofa I had ever sat on. Obviously NSC officers wanted for nothing. So what was wrong with me? Why couldn't I just accept what I had and what millions would love to have? Maybe I just needed a dose of reality. Well, I knew someone who could give me that.

I punched in Max Creeling's number on the tablet. I knew it was equipped to allow me to see anyone I called. But that presupposed that the other person had an equally advanced piece of tech to speak into. Max had an antique flip-top phone, which I knew would only have about five minutes of credits.

"Hello," a voice said suspiciously.

"Hi," I said.

"Hi, buddy! How the heck are you?" Max said, recognizing me.

"That's NSC officer First Class Duran to you."

"Wow! Wow! Wow! You got it!"

"Piece of cake."

"So tell me all about it. How many people were there going for it? What did you have to do? I've got so many questions."

"First let's talk about you, Max. How's Seattle? Have you been staying away from casinos?"

"Boring—and yes. When have I ever let you down?"

"Well…"

"Okay, okay, don't answer that. I may have done, just a couple of times, but I haven't placed a bet since I got here. Cross my heart and hope to die."

"Good man. So you think you can lay low there for a few more weeks?"

"Of course," Max said. He hesitated. He had picked up something was wrong. "You sure you're okay?"

"Why wouldn't I be, Max?"

"No reason, I guess."

"I just want to get settled in and take care of a few things first. I'll call you in a couple of days, okay?"

"Okay, buddy, and great work. I'm proud of you."

Max's phone clicked off. I sat back against the chair. I knew I'd been a wimp. I hadn't told Max anything. What was up with me? That was a question I'd been mulling over far too much since I'd put on the NSC uniform.

I sat back in the desk chair. Was I really prepared to just ignore everything that went on here and "live the life?" I really would be crazy to give it all up, wouldn't I?

I stared at the tablet. Back in the day, these things were capable of answering even the most difficult question. So how did I get this one to talk? There was a small globe at the top of the tablet screen. I pressed it.

The words "How can I help you?" came up on the screen and were simultaneously spoken by a soft-voiced female.

"Question," I said.

"Identification," the voice said.

"Duran, Hogan. Officer First Class. Code thirty-three ninety-nine."

"Voice recognized. Code accepted. Access granted."

"What's your name?"

"Segovia."

"Segovia, search Gunner, Roy."

Instantly a younger, clean-cut photo of Hunter appeared on the tablet screen.

"Gunner, Roy. Commander. NSC First Class. Security level seven," Segovia said.

"Current status?"

"Deceased."

"Search, Mason, Ruby."

A recent photo of Ruby replaced Hunter's picture.

"Mason, Ruby. Candidate Finalist," Segovia confirmed.

"Access mainframe."

"Authorization code?"

I hesitated. I didn't have that code.

"Access denied," Segovia said quickly. The tablet screen turned black.

Well, Segovia wasn't half as compliant as I thought she would be. But a plan was starting to form.

I got up. I had work to do.

CHAPTER SIXTEEN

I SAUNTERED DOWN THE CORRIDOR TOWARD the chamber room door, marveling again at how every single detail of the complex seemed to have been faithfully and exactly copied in the virtual reality world.

"Evening, Officer Duran," a voice said.

Surprised, I turned to face a hovering glider ball. General Stoker's face stared out at me.

"Where are you going, soldier?"

"Couldn't sleep, sir. Commander Beecham suggested I try a training program."

"You know where it is?"

"Yes, sir, near the canteen."

"Correct. First left, straight ahead for three hundred yards, right, second left, and then first right. Have fun."

The ball shot off, back up the corridor. I waited until it had disappeared around the corner and then moved closer to the chamber room door.

"Duran, Hogan," I said, glancing around.

The corridor was empty, but I felt as if someone was watching me.

The door slid open. No one seemed to be inside. I quickly walked towards the row of chambers where I'd seen Ruby. She was still there, floating naked with her eyes closed.

I pulled at my uniform, taking it off rapidly and dumping it on the floor. Naked, I opened Ruby's chamber door and stepped in. The door behind me sealed tight and my feet left the ground as I started to float. Now came the really difficult bit.

I had assumed that if I just stood in the chamber and closed my eyes I could join Ruby in the VR program. As I waited, I knew that what happened in the next few minutes would determine the rest of my life. My fate at the NSC had been sealed by lying to Stoker and entering the chamber room without permission.

Now there was no going back. My short career as an NSC officer was over.

Why was nothing happening?

I opened my eyes and looked at Ruby. It was disconcerting floating so close to a beautiful naked woman. I saw Ruby's hand tighten. If she was in the world I thought she was in things were probably not going well.

I reached across and held Ruby's hand, trying to soothe her. She gripped me tightly, and as she did, I closed my eyes again and the chamber disappeared. It was replaced by the mainframe room.

Jackpot! I had entered Ruby's reality, where Stoker had said *I* was the symbiote, the traitor.

I looked down. I was now dressed as a candidate and was hidden behind a bank of servers. From here I could see my symbiote-self had a gun to Ruby's head. Commander Beecham lay on the floor unconscious. There was no sign of Systems Analyst Rodriguez.

I could hear people banging on the door outside. Obviously Ruby was under attack from the Krails and had retreated to the mainframe room to try and defend herself. This was the same as my story, but one with a different ending. In this new narrative, Ruby looked like she would be killed, and the Krail traitor, me, would win.

My Krail-self pushed his gun even harder into Ruby's forehead. "Just enter the codes," he said. "You know the Krail way is the only way." His finger tightened on the trigger as I crept up and drove my fist into his head.

Krail Hogan dropped the gun and fell to the floor. He looked up and saw me, the real Hogan, standing over him.

"Who are you? Did those bastards *clone* me?" Krail Hogan said as he reached down to his belt. Pulling a knife out, he jumped to his feet and lunged at me. I took a step to my right. The knife narrowly missed as Ruby dived to the floor and picked up Krail Hogan's gun.

"Ruby, help me!" I shouted as my doppelganger swiped down with his knife but again failed to make contact.

Ruby swung the gun between him and me. She had no idea which one of us she should shoot.

Outside, the banging and shouting reached a crescendo. The door finally gave way under the weight of the Krail hordes. It fell to the floor with an ear-splitting crash.

Distracted, Krail Hogan swung around as Hunter charged in, followed by a pack of screaming Krails. I saw my chance and yanked Krail Hogan's arms down, knocking his knife away.

Krail Hogan, a look of hate in his eyes, shouted out, "I'm going to kill you, bast—" A thick muscular arm wrapped around his neck.

I lowered my fists and watched Hunter push Krail Hogan to his knees. Moments later I was grabbed by Krails. Others headed for Ruby. She waved her gun in an arc as she retreated from them.

"Get back or I'll shoot!" she shouted.

"Let them both go," Hunter ordered as he continued to hold on tight to Krail Hogan.

The confused Krails hesitated.

"I said leave them!" Hunter shouted.

"You heard him. Back off, assholes," Ruby said defiantly.

Reluctantly, the Krails released me and stepped away from Ruby.

"Wreckage. Tabika." Hunter pointed at two of the Krails. "Tie this one up and take him away."

He pushed Krail Hogan forward into the arms of the Krails.

"Now the rest of you go," Hunter ordered.

The confused Krails looked at one another, unsure what to do.

"Boss, do you really want them to leave?" Wreckage yanked a rope tight around Krail Hogan's hands.

"What's wrong with you all?" Hunter asked. "You got a problem with your hearing?"

Wreckage shrugged. "Do what the boss says," he told the others. "Go."

The Krails began to stream out. Wreckage and Tabika followed, pushing Krail Hogan ahead of them.

"Why are you doing this, Hunter?" Krail Hogan shouted. "He's the clone," he said, indicating me.

Wreckage hit Krail Hogan hard. "The boss wants you out, so you're going out."

"You put your gun down too, Ruby," Hunter said.

"Not until you tell me what the hell's going on."

"Nothing you see here is real, Ruby… Right, Hogan?"

"Yeah, Ruby, you are simply part of a giant, living VR program." I glanced across at Hunter. "You know that too, right?"

"Sure. I practically designed this program myself."

"Do your men know?"

"Some do. Others suspect."

"So why do you play? You could get killed in here."

"For every Krail that finds out and refuses to take part in the game, ten other Krails are removed from the diamond mine and killed." Hunter walked past me and toward Ruby.

Ruby looked from the Krail leader to me. It was hard for her to take all this in. Everything around her looked absolutely real so she was unwilling to put down her weapon.

"Get back," she ordered. "This is all bullshit. Diamond mines? I have no idea why the two of you are talking crap, but how about I prove it by shooting you, and then we'll see what's real." Ruby pointed her gun directly at Hunter.

Hunter reached into his pocket.

"Hey, easy. What are you doing?" Ruby said.

"Just showing you something." He took out a huge diamond and lifted it to the light. "This came from the mine."

Open-mouthed, Ruby stared at the sparkling gem as the big Krail reached across, grabbed the gun from her, and threw it in the air. It disappeared.

"Bullshit, huh," Hunter said. "See? Now there's no gun."

"He's telling the truth," I said. "We *are* in a simulation. It's been set up to find out if you're qualified to join the NSC."

"So why were there two of you in here, Hogan?" asked Ruby.

"To save you. To save you from me."

Ruby shook her head. "You're full of it. I didn't need your help."

"What? My doppelganger wasn't about to kill you, then?"

"No," Ruby said slowly.

"For Christ sake, can you two stop bickering and listen?" Hunter said. "We've only a few minutes before someone notices that this program has come to an end. Hogan, explain to her why you came back here."

"I wanted to talk to Hunter, Ruby. His real name is Roy Gunner. He's an ex-NSC officer, though according to the records, he's deceased. Right?"

"Yes. Of course, I'm dead. I got a funeral with full honors. The NSC doesn't like to advertise their failures. But they all have to go. The organization has to be destroyed."

"What? Why?" asked Ruby.

"Because the diamond mines are just part of it. All the money the NSC vacuums up goes to them and their masters. It's the fluid they use to oil the mechanism to concentrate all power into a tiny wealthy elite group. All of the rest go hungry because they know that a starving world is easier to rule," Hunter said.

"You really believe this, Hogan?"

"I…I don't know. But there's something not right. And there definitely is a diamond mine. I've seen it," I said, as the room began to shake.

"What's happening?" Ruby exclaimed.

"I told you. The program's ending. We need to destroy the base. I can do that with your help and get you out of this place. But I need you to—" Hunter began.

There was a blinding flash of light.

CHAPTER
SEVENTEEN

"WELCOME HOME, RUBY. YOU TOO, Duran," a voice said.

I opened my eyes. I was lying naked in the chamber next to an equally naked Ruby. The chamber's door was open and Jake Teerman stared down at us. He was dressed in an NSC officer's uniform.

Jake pushed his hand out to help Ruby up. She ignored it, stood, and then fell back against the chamber wall.

"You okay?" I got to my feet.

"Just feeling a bit dizzy."

"Happened to me, too, the first time. It's from the VR immersion. You'll be okay in a few moments."

"He's right, Ruby. Just take your time," Jake said.

"What are you doing here?" I asked.

"The same as you, Duran. I'm learning all about the wonderful world of being an NSC officer."

"You got in?"

"Of course. You didn't think I'd fail, did you?"

"Could someone get me some clothes, please?" Ruby asked.

"Teerman, make yourself useful. Find Ruby something to wear." I stepped out of the chamber and picked up my discarded officer's uniform.

"Already there, Duran." He threw a blue coverall at Ruby. "There you go." Jake smiled broadly. "Personally, though, I prefer you *au naturale.*"

Ruby scowled at him and started to dress.

"You still haven't told me why you're here." I pulled my pants on.

"When I saw you enter the chamber room I guessed you were going back to get Ruby."

"You've been following me?"

"Maybe."

"And why would you do that?"

"I figured that you'd be thinking of giving up and leaving. I knew you'd develop a conscience about the Krails when you found out the way the NSC really operates."

"That doesn't bother you?"

Jake shook his head. "Of course not. I just got the perfect job, and now I can live a life of luxury. So, no, I don't care about any of it."

"Well, I do."

"Of course you do. You're a sensitive soul," Jake said sarcastically. "That's why I'm here."

"Oh, really?" A now-dressed Ruby stepped out of the chamber.

"Yes, I thought we could help each other."

"And how would we do that?" I asked.

Jake moved closer. "I got out of VR a couple of days ago, and I've been spending my time collecting these." He produced a handful of diamonds from his pocket. They sparkled in the light. "They're worth a fortune, but they're no use to me in here. And if I tried to smuggle them out and got caught I'd lose everything. So I need someone to do that for me. Someone like *you*, Duran."

"But why would I help you, Teerman? I could just tell Beecham I don't think the job's for me and then leave—without the risk of being caught with those stones."

Jake laughed. "That's a good one. You're a real joker, Duran. You'll just ask to leave!" He stared hard at me. "No, they'd never let you do it. You'd both go right back into VR and this time, they'll never let you out. All I have to do is press that." Jake pointed to an alarm on the wall.

"The NSC would do that to us?" Ruby asked.

"Without hesitation. And that's your best option. They could just decide to shoot you and be done," Jake said. "But the alternative is I can help you escape, and we can all be rich."

"How do you know we wouldn't just take the diamonds and disappear?"

"Because I know you, Duran. You're honorable." Jake sneered.

I stared at him. "Can Ruby and I talk this over?"

"You're not seriously considering this," Ruby said, horrified.

"He's offering us a way out."

Jake glanced around. "We haven't got much time. I'll give you five seconds to decide. Four. Three. Two…"

"I'll do it!" I said. "Now let me take look at those." I reached across and swiped the diamonds out of Jake's hand. "Oops!"

"You asshole!" Jake bent down, scrabbling to pick up the precious stones.

I reached over and pressed the alarm.

The Klaxon wailed and wailed. Moments later the chamber room door slid open, and two officers rushed in, their guns drawn.

"What's going on?" one of them shouted, staring at Jake picking up the gems from the floor.

"Thank God!" I yelled. "He's stealing diamonds!"

"You. Up. Now!" the other officer yelled as both men ran toward Jake.

I grabbed Ruby's hand. "Go!" I said. "Let's see how far my honor gets us this time."

We hurried away from the chamber room. We both knew we only had a short time before Jake convinced the officers that it was not him but us who had stolen the gemstones.

"Down there." I pointed to an empty corridor to the left.

We walked quickly on, following the passageway as it curved to the right.

"Damn." Ruby stopped. The corridor ahead came to a dead end, blocked by a concrete wall. She turned to retrace her steps.

"Wait." I grabbed her arm. "Maybe we can get out through that." I pointed to a small window cut into the bricks. I walked over to it, jammed my hands under the frame and tried to push it open. But it wouldn't budge.

"Need some help?" Ruby joined me. "On the count of three. One. Two. Three. Push!"

The window slowly opened, and I leaned out. We were about fifty feet above the ground. Below, searchlights swung back and forth over a concrete square. I twisted my body around and looked up. A flat roof was fifteen feet or so above us.

That was the way to go.

Ruby went out the window first. She slid over the ledge and stretched to grasp onto the crumbling red brick wall. Following, I pulled myself out and climbed after her.

It took us several minutes to reach the top, but we finally made it.

"So, what next?" Ruby stood up on the tiled roof.

"I doubt if we can get out of this place on our own. We need help." I paused. "I think we need the Krails."

"Sure. Why don't I just whistle and see if they come running to rescue us? The last time I saw them, they were after my blood."

"Right, but I know someone who can get them on our side."

Ruby stared at me. "You want to rescue Hunter, don't you?"

"Hunter said he could get us out."

"He did, but he's back in the chamber room, and returning there would be like walking into the lion's den."

"So have you a better plan?"

Ruby thought for a moment. Then: "Not currently. No."

We walked across the roof until we reached the edge of the building. A gap of twelve feet or so lay between where we stood and the next unit. Looking down, I realized that we'd actually been climbing and there was now a drop of around eighty feet to the ground.

Ruby tapped me on the shoulder. "Look," she said.

I turned. Pinpricks of light were visible in the distance. They were moving toward us.

"Are those flashlights?"

"I think so. Come on, we have to jump," I said. "Ready?"

"What? Over there? No way!"

"If we don't, they're going to get us." I ran toward the gap.

I had no idea if I would make it, but as I flew through air, I felt a rush of adrenalin and a surge of exhilaration. If I was going to die, I was going to die happy.

The jump could only have lasted a few seconds, but by the time my feet landed on the roof, it felt like eternity. I looked around for Ruby. She was still hanging back on the other side.

"Jump!" I shouted.

Ruby glanced around at our pursuers. They were closer now: two officers—a man and a woman, their guns out. Ruby took a deep breath and started to run, faster and faster.

Then she leapt.

Ruby cleared the gap and landed on the very edge of the building. Her smile vanished as she lost her footing. I reached out and grabbed her arm just as she was about to fall. I yanked her toward me. For a moment we both forgot where we were and stared into each other's eyes. Then we heard the shouts of our pursuers.

We started to run again, trying to put as much distance between them and us as possible.

"They're not going to make that jump," I said. "Only idiots like us would do that."

Ruby looked back. "I think you may be wrong about that."

I turned. The female officer was readying to leap across the chasm.

We ran on until we reached the edge of the unit. We were now almost a hundred feet above the ground, and this time there was no other building to jump to.

I felt movement under my feet. "What was that?" I asked.

"I think the roof's tipping!" Ruby sat down.

"Come on. We can slide to the ground."

The tiles shredded our clothes and tore into our flesh as we slid forward, moving faster and faster.

A shout came from above. I twisted my head. The two officers were slithering down after us.

Turning, I saw that the ground was getting ever closer. If we continued at this speed, we would die when we hit it.

"Brake!" I pushed my shoes down hard on the tiles.

Behind, the officers were almost upon us. A fat man appeared just to my right. Smiling, he pulled out his gun, pointed it at me, and steadied his aim.

On the other side, the woman officer had drawn next to Ruby. Grinning maniacally, she mouthed a silent farewell as she pressed the trigger on her gun. Ruby kicked out, hitting her hard on her side. She spun around, and the bullet flew harmlessly into the air. Undaunted, the officer pulled her weapon back and aimed it again at Ruby.

"Duck!" I screamed. We both bent forward as the woman's bullet flew over Ruby's head. Simultaneously, the fat officer fired. His bullet struck the woman at the same time as her bullet hit him. Both screamed in agony as blood spurted from their wounds.

They continued to slide down, moving past us at high speed before smashing into the ground—the impact killing them instantly.

"Head for her, Ruby!" I shouted, pointing to the dead woman officer and moving to position myself above the fat officer's body.

Reaching the bottom, my feet dug into the man and twisted him around just as Ruby crashed into the woman.

We stood up slowly, happy to be on solid ground and alive.

"How do you feel?" Ruby rubbed her legs.

"Like I've just been run over by a truck." I picked up the female officer's gun and threw it to Ruby. "Keep that." I pushed the man's weapon into the waistband of my pants.

"You still want to go to the chamber room?" Ruby asked.

"We've got no choice. We need Hunter."

CHAPTER EIGHTEEN

THE SUN WAS PEEKING OVER the horizon as we headed for the main fortress. We stuck close to the brick building, constantly checking for officers and cameras. But the area looked like it was rarely visited; weeds stuck out through the cracked brown earth.

Reaching the end of the wall, I stared out. Open desolate land lay ahead. "What do you think?" Ruby asked.

I hesitated. To be honest, I thought we stood little chance of reaching either the chamber room or escaping from the base. "I don't know. It doesn't look good."

I leaned against the building. "I think we have to take the chance and run." "Okay, ready?" Ruby said.

I nodded, but then as she was about to run, I grabbed her. "Hey. Wait a minute! Take a look at those weeds."

Ruby stared at me. "Hogan, you're losing it. This is no time to think about gardening."

"No, look. You see the strange way they're growing? They're spread evenly—except in that area," I said, pointing.

Ruby bent down. "You're right." She passed her hands over the ground. "The soil doesn't match its surroundings, either."

She scooped up the dirt and ran it through her fingers. "It's really fine." She moved her hand backward and forward. "I think there's something under here."

For the next few minutes we frantically brushed at the dirt, uncovering what looked like a large metal manhole plate.

"Why would that be out here?" I asked.

"I don't know. Help me lever it up."

We both pushed our fingers under the cover and tried to lift the plate, but it wouldn't budge.

"Perhaps it's locked from inside," Ruby said.

"Maybe." I leaned in and stared at two small indentations in the center of the plate. I put my finger in one. It didn't fit. I tried my thumb instead. That slotted in perfectly.

"Try your other thumb too," Ruby said.

I kept one thumb in one indentation and put my other thumb in the second indentation.

Nothing happened.

"Do you think these indents have got anything to do with anything?" Ruby asked.

"I don't know. Why don't you try?"

Ruby repeated what I had done without success.

"This is a waste of time. Let's go." I stood.

Ruby remained seated and continued to stare at the cover. "How about you try placing your thumb in one indentation, and I'll put mine in the other."

I sighed. "Okay, it's worth a try."

We each placed a thumb in the indentations. After a moment we heard a ticking sound.

"Hear that?" said Ruby, excited. The noise suddenly stopped. "Damn," she murmured, deflated. "Just when I thought we were getting somewhere."

I continued to stare at the metal plate. There was one absurd possibility. I got up quickly and pulled Ruby back. "It's going to blow," I said.

"What?"

"Move away."

Ruby took a few hesitant steps back. We waited.

Again nothing happened.

"Okay, you're right. Now I really feel like an idiot."

I took a pace forward just as the cover blew off and flew into the air. I dove to the ground. The metal plate landed inches from my head.

Ruby helped me up. "That's a pretty stupid way to open something," she said.

Cautiously we walked back to the manhole and stared down. A set of metal stairs ran on one side of the hole. LED spots lined the other side of the shaft, illuminating the stairs.

"I can't see the ground, can you?"

Ruby shook her head. "So what do you think?"

I stroked my chin. "We have to get to the chamber room, but that looks virtually impossible if we stay above ground, so…"

"We go down," said Ruby decisively.

CHAPTER NINETEEN

W E CLAMBERED DOWN THE METAL stairs. Ruby counted over five hundred steps before we reached the ground. A long tunnel stretched to the east. It was about ten feet high—its walls were steel plated, its floor lined with gray concrete.

"Do you think it connects to the main base?" I asked.

"Where else would it go?" She set off down the tunnel.

We had been walking for about five minutes when I heard the sound. At first, I ignored it, figuring my ears must be playing tricks on me.

"Ruby?" I said finally. "Can you hear that?"

"The scratching noise?"

I nodded. "Yeah. It seems to be getting louder. We need to get out of here."

We increased our pace. Soon we'd given up any pretense of walking and were both running, but it was no use. The noise got louder and closer. We kept looking back but couldn't see anything.

"There." I pointed ahead at a dot of light on the side of the corridor about seven feet above the ground. It was yellow, unlike the white overhead LED lights.

Ruby squinted. "What is it?"

"I don't know." I pulled my gun out. "But get ready. Whatever or whoever's making that noise behind us is moving faster than we are."

As we ran on, we saw that the yellow light came from a lamp positioned over a large steel door.

"Thank god. A way out," Ruby said.

I glanced back. "Jeez, look!" Finally, I saw what had been chasing us. A V-shaped army of rats had appeared around the bend of the corridor. They were running toward us.

I sprinted the last few feet to the door and tried to turn the handle, but it was locked.

The rodents were now only about two hundred yards away. A massive black rat the size of a small dog led the seething brown mass.

"Try shooting, Ruby, maybe that will slow them down." I studied the door.

As Ruby fired at the rats, I moved my palm over the metal looking for a way to open the door. I felt two slight indentations at waist height. "Got something!"

"Good, because this isn't working."

I turned. Ruby was firing, and dead rats were dropping to the ground. But the others just continued on, running over their compatriots as they advanced.

I placed my thumb in one of the indentations. "Ruby, help me!"

She swung around.

"Put your thumb next to mine. You'll feel the indentation. Maybe this will work the way it did with the manhole cover."

As Ruby obeyed, I looked back down the corridor. The entire rodent army had suddenly come to a halt. They were lining up behind the huge lead rat.

"It's not opening," Ruby said, exasperated.

"Useless." I took my thumb away just as the leader rat broke away from the pack and sprinted toward us.

We both fired at him, but it was futile. The monstrous rodent seemed to anticipate the path of our bullets and swerved from one side to the other to avoid them.

Ruby's gun clicked. It was empty. She screamed as she threw the gun down and stepped back—through the open entrance. "Hogan!"

I turned. The door had slid to one side. The massive rat leapt at me. His mouth wide open, revealing long yellow teeth. I pushed my hands up to protect my neck and stepped back just as the portal slid closed!

From outside I heard a dull thump as the huge rat crashed harmlessly against the steel door.

The white-walled room we had entered was the chamber room.

Somehow we'd doubled back on ourselves; the NSC facility really was a maze. Parallel rows of chambers stretched far into the distance. Lines of steel lockers reaching from the floor to the ceiling stood on either side of the door. I opened one. They were filled with coveralls, the same coveralls Ruby was wearing.

I grabbed Ruby's hand. "Come on. Let's check it out."

We walked down the nearest line of chambers. Each of the enclosed containers held a naked Krail.

"There must be hundreds of them," I whispered.

"Yeah," said Ruby quietly. "Let's find Hunter."

We walked down the first and the second row but there was no sign of the Krail leader. Ruby stopped. "Hogan, if we don't find him soon, we'll have no choice but to try and escape on our own."

"Fine."

We walked on, but we still couldn't see Hunter.

I spotted him just as we were about to give up. He was in a chamber midway down the eighth line. "That's him, right?"

"Yes, I think so." Ruby stared into the chamber containing a large naked Krail. "But last time I saw Hunter he was dressed. What now?"

"We go back in the program and connect." I started to take off my clothes.

"What are you…?"

"We have to be naked to travel, Ruby."

"Well, when in Rome." She pulled off her coveralls.

After piling our clothes up, we climbed into Hunter's chamber. It was a tight fit. The chamber wasn't designed for three people.

I pressed my body hard against the wall, and Ruby did the same on the other side. Together we sandwiched Hunter. He floated with his eyes closed, his breathing slow and shallow.

"I didn't sign up for this, Hogan."

"Neither did he."

"Now what?"

"We both grab his hand."

Ruby took one of Hunter's hands, while I took the other. It was cold and inert.

"Close your eyes," I said.

"I've been expecting you," a deep voice announced.

I flicked my eyes open.

I was crouched in a large cave lit by flaming torches. Hunter sat opposite.

"You were?" I noticed that I was now dressed as a candidate.

"I knew you'd try to find me, but I wasn't sure you'd make it."

"Thanks for the vote of confidence," I said. "Have you seen—"

"Boss," a voice said, interrupting.

I turned. The Krail called Wreckage stood at the entrance to the cave and held a gun to Ruby's head. She too was now dressed as a candidate.

"I found this one creeping around outside," Wreckage said.

"Can you call this big lug off, please?" Ruby looked directly at Hunter.

"Let her go," the Krail leader ordered.

"You sure, Boss?"

"Do it!"

Wreckage lowered his weapon.

"And you can leave now."

"Right, Boss." Wreckage walked out of the cave.

Hunter smiled at Ruby. "Sorry about that. He's an excellent soldier but not the sharpest tool in the box." He paused. "Welcome back."

"Hogan convinced me to come."

"So do you believe me now? About the NSC?"

"Maybe."

"I think you do. That's why you risked everything to come here. But are you willing to take the first step to destroy the organization?"

"How?" I asked.

"By blowing up the base and everything in it."

"You want to kill everyone," said Ruby, horrified.

"Of course not. There will be time for all the Krails to leave."

"And the NSC members?" I asked.

"Those that have any sense will escape before the buildings go up, but the diehard officers will probably be prepared to go down with the ship."

"You're willing to go along with this, Hogan? You believe what Hunter says about the NSC? I thought the plan was just for us to escape?"

"Hunter," I said, "you really can get us out of the base?"

"Yes, if you help me."

"And can you prove that the NSC is a totally corrupt organization set up to only protect the rich?" I asked.

"Hogan, I have it all documented—their every dirty little secret. Bank account numbers, assassinations, the mass poverty program...the lot."

"So why haven't you used this proof a long time ago?" asked Ruby.

"I can't access it. It's hidden in the program. They killed me off, removed all my clearances, and changed all the security codes. But Hogan, you have the new codes."

"I have one code," I said, "but I don't know if it will still work."

"Try," Hunter said.

"What? Here in this cave?"

"It's not a cave. It's an edifice created within the program. Say the code."

"Okay, here goes." Raising my voice, I spoke to the empty cave. "NSC officer Duran, Hogan. Fort-five, forty-five dash nine. Authorization code three-two-two-Bravo-twenty-nine. Requesting access to program." I stopped. "Now what?"

Hunter suddenly lunged for me, grabbing my head on both sides.

There was an intense white light, and streams and streams of numbers and information appeared in front of me. Then another bright flash of light almost blinded me.

The cave disappeared, and I flew through the air, out of the open chamber door, and fell to the floor. I was now naked. A naked Ruby lay a few feet away. Hunter was sprawled next to her. He was unconscious and naked too.

"Here, put these on," a voice demanded.

I looked up, trying to focus my eyes, and saw Commander Beecham with an NSC officer. Both had their guns out.

Beecham threw coveralls onto the floor. "You really must learn to keep your kit on, Duran. You too, Mason," Beecham said as I reached for the clothes.

While we dressed, the commander walked across to the still unconscious Hunter. He stared down at him and then kicked him hard in his stomach. "Wake up, Hunter—or should I say Gunner?"

Hunter didn't move. Beecham kicked him a second time, his black military boot smashing into the large man's ribs.

"Leave him alone, you asshole," Ruby said.

"Look who's got her mojo back." Beecham stared down at the unconscious Hunter. "It seems that your friend's journey back may have been a bit much for him. Unsurprising, really. It's been years since he's been here, in the real world."

He turned his gaze on us. "You two have caused a lot of trouble." Beecham walked across and tapped my head. "Is it all up there now?"

Ruby glanced over at me. Beecham saw the look. "You're thinking, how do I know that? Well, let me enlighten you. You take that sort of information off the mainframe and all kinds of alarms go off. How do you think we found you so quickly?"

"Is it true what Hunter said?"

"Of course it is, Mason. In this world, there are only two sorts of people—lions and sheep. The lions, of whom there are relatively few, are always destined to rule over the poor sheep. Duran's decided he's going to be a sheep after all." Beecham pulled his gun round and pointed it at my head. "A shame," he said. "Any last words?"

"Fuck you." I dove at Beecham. The commander moved back quickly, his finger tightening on the trigger.

"Nice try, Duran, but—"A hand reached out, grabbed Beecham's leg and yanked him to the floor. His gun spun into the air. Simultaneously, Ruby launched herself at the guard, her feet flying forward, knocking the man to the ground.

I grabbed Beecham's pistol as Ruby scooped up the officer's weapon. She pointed it at the man.

"You, face down. Now!"

The officer rolled onto his front as Hunter stood and pulled on a set of coveralls.

"You okay?" I asked.

"I've got a raging headache, and my body feels like shit—but besides that, I feel good, *really* good." He drove his heel hard into Beecham's midsection.

The commander groaned and spat. "You don't honestly think you can get out of here. If I don't leave this room, soon there'll be scores of people coming to look for me."

Hunter leaned down. "Sleep tight." He smashed his fist against Beecham's head.

"What now?" Ruby asked.

"Beecham's right, isn't he, Hunter?" I said.

The big Krail nodded. "Unfortunately he is, although I think we've still got a couple of minutes before more men come down. That's plenty of time to get this place ready to blow."

"How?" I asked.

"We just need the right code. It'll trigger the self-destruct sequence. You have it, Hogan."

"I don't. I've given you the only code I had. What about him?" I pointed at Beecham. "He'll know it, won't he?"

"Perhaps," Hunter said. "But whatever you think about Beecham, he'll be a tough nut to crack, and we certainly wouldn't be able to make him talk before help arrives."

"What about this one?" Ruby pointed at the cowering officer.

"Too low down on the totem pole. He's just assigned to guard the chamber room."

"So why would you think I would have the code? I was just a lowly NSC officer too," I said.

"Specifically, you've just become an NSC officer," Hunter said.

"So?"

"It's part of their game," Hunter told me. "When a new officer joins up, they give them the new termination code without telling them that's what it is. I guess it keeps things interesting for the higher-ups."

"That doesn't make sense."

"Most times, life on this base is pretty boring. Stoker and Beecham get their kicks from knowing that the newbie has the means to destroy the entire complex on their first day if they wanted to. Of course, they never ever thought that it would happen."

"You said 'on their first day?'"

"The code is changed daily."

"So Hogan, you should be able to work it out, right?" Hunter glanced across at the door. "And you better do it quickly. People will be down here very soon."

I put my hands to my head. What could the code be? I had been shown around, spoken to Max… "I've got nothing."

"There's been no time over the past day when someone hasn't asked you to remember some form of word code?"

"Think hard!" Ruby said. "You can do this, Hogan."

"No." I shook my head. "No there's nothing. Except…"

What had Beecham said in the diamond mine? *Oh, and here's something you may want to remember. Every mine we open, we open on Level 21.*

"Computer, NSC Officer Duran, Hogan. Prepare for termination. Termination code Level Twenty-one."

Lights began to flash overhead as a Klaxon started up.

"Attention. Attention. Termination in fifteen minutes. Evacuate compound. Termination in fifteen minutes," a female computerized voice announced over the speaker system.

"Good work!" Hunter smiled.

"A lucky guess."

From behind came the sound of the chamber doors sliding open.

"Ruby, can you guard the entrance while Hogan and I get the Krails out?" Hunter said.

"Sure. Send them over for clothes."

Ignoring the unconscious Beecham, Ruby ordered the guard up to open the lockers.

Meantime, Hunter and I set about releasing the Krails from the chambers.

CHAPTER
TWENTY

T ABIKA WAS ONE OF THE first to get out. He, like Hunter, knew that he had been living in a Virtual Reality World so his "awakening" wasn't as traumatic as it was for the others. Hunter instructed Tabika to take a small team of men to find and free the Krails working underground in the diamond mines.

"Do whatever's necessary!" Hunter ordered.

Most of the other Krails came out of their chambers blinking and confused. Neither of us had time to explain where they were or what was happening, but since their leader was obviously in charge they trusted implicitly that all would soon be made clear.

Leaving Hunter to ensure all the remaining Krails were released, I returned to take care of Commander Beecham. Although he still appeared to be unconscious, I wasn't taking any chances. I stuffed a coverall into his mouth and twisted the cloth-arms around the back of his head, tying them tight. Then, pulling his arms around his back and twisting another coverall over his hands, I bound the commander securely.

Beecham's eyes opened as I was finishing. He tried to say something, but the gag stopped him from talking.

"How is he?" Ruby shouted from across the room, where Krails were dressing.

"Awake." I pulled Beecham roughly to his feet.

I pushed the commander toward the door. Krails turned to stare aggressively at him. All knew about Beecham and were itching to rip him apart. Some started to move forward.

"Hunter, I need you here!" I shouted.

The Krail leader appeared from behind a line of chambers. He saw his men advancing toward Beecham.

"Back off!" Hunter strode toward his men. "That's an order."

Wreckage stepped from behind Hunter and placed himself in front of Beecham. "You heard the boss. Back off."

Muttering, the Krails halted.

"We have to move soon," Ruby said. "Are all the chambers empty now?"

"Yep, everyone's out." Hunter held up his hand. "Listen up, everyone. I know you are all confused and unsure what is happening, but you have to trust me. You have been living inside a nightmare, one that will soon be over."

Behind, I leaned across to Hunter. "You sure he'll come?" I asked quietly.

"He has to. I told you, he could only stop the termination from the same room where it began—this room. Those are the rules. So yeah, he'll turn up. It's your plan I'm not so sure about."

"It'll work, trust me." Though to be honest, I knew there was probably only a fifty-fifty chance it would, but it was better than nothing.

The chamber room door suddenly slid open to reveal General Stoker leading a squad of armed officers.

The Krails stared at them as Stoker's eyes fixed on me.

"So, Duran, decided to switch sides, have we?"

"Termination in twelve minutes," the computer voice said.

"And you're going to blow us all up too. How noble."

"It's over, Stoker. Your whole rotten little empire. Tell your men to put down their weapons and they can go free."

General Stoker turned to his troops and smiled. "Hawthorne," he said to an officer standing to behind him. "Order the men to take positions."

"Lock arms," came the command from Officer Hawthorne, followed by the ominous clicks of dozens of weapons being readied.

"Duran, these men are the NSC's elite of the elite. Those degenerates will stand no chance." General Stoker indicated the massed Krails. "Do you really want their deaths on your conscience?"

"I take your point, General. But I ask you, do you really want Commander Beecham's death on yours?" I raised my gun to Beecham's head. "Be reasonable, General. It's over."

"Terminating in eleven minutes."

Stoker smiled. "Maybe you do have a point." He stroked his chin. "Commander Beecham's life for our surrender?"

He moved his gun around and shot the guard standing by the lockers. He fell screaming to the floor.

Stoker pulled his gun back to point at Beecham. "Officers captured by the enemy know to accept their fate. Goodbye, Commander."

The general fired, hitting Beecham in the face. He was dead before he reached the ground.

"I told you he wouldn't surrender." Hunter snatched my gun and raised it to shoot. Stoker slid behind his troops as the Krail leader fired.

The officers raised their shields. Hunter's bullet bounced harmlessly off them.

The Krail threw his gun down in frustration. "Charge!" Hunter shouted.

We all ran screaming towards the NSC squad. The troops fired into the advancing army of unarmed men. It seemed like suicide, but I for one didn't care. I was going to die fighting. All around me Krails fell—bloodied, dead, or wounded.

But that didn't stop us, and soon the sheer numbers of Krails started to overwhelm the NSC officers. However well trained they were, they didn't stand a chance against the pure ferocity of the Krails' attack.

General Stoker wasn't about to die in the horde, however. He backed off and broke away, attempting to vanish in the thick of the battle.

Wrenching a gun out of the hands of a dead officer, I headed after him. Ruby followed.

"He went over there!" I pointed to the second row of empty chambers.

Together Ruby and I ran down the line.

"Termination in nine minutes. You have nine minutes left to evacuate the complex. Leave now!" the computer announced.

"Hogan, we've got to get out of here," Ruby said.

"Not before we find that bastard."

"But we've only got a few minutes and everything blows!"

"Let me help you then," a voice said.

I swung around to face General Stoker. He had his gun pointing directly at Ruby's head.

"Put the weapon down, Duran, or I'll blow her brains out."

"Shoot him, Hogan!" she shouted.

I hesitated and shook my head. "No, I'm not like him, Ruby." I dropped my gun to the floor.

"Good man," Stoker said. "Now let's deal with this termination problem."

"Authorization Stoker. Seven-nine-three-three-six-four-two. Override termination."

"Voice recognized. Level Nine Security access granted. Clearance code?" the computer asked.

Stoker smiled. "Level Twenty-One." He waited.

"Clearance Code not recognized."

"What? That's impossible. I said Level Twenty-One," Stoker yelled.

"Repeat. Clearance Code not recognized. Termination in eight minutes."

"Now!" I shouted to Ruby.

She spun around and grasped Stoker's gun. The weapon fired, just missing her leg as I kicked the pistol out of the general's hand. It flew through the air and landed about ten feet from me.

Stoker launched himself forward and grabbed at my discarded pistol. He brought it around and aimed it at me.

"Goodbye, Officer Duran. It's been nice knowing you." Suddenly, he was screaming in agony. He dropped the gun and spun around to reveal an axe embedded in his back. Hunter stood behind him.

The general fell backward onto the floor, blood gushing from his wound.

Ruby got up and stared at Stoker's dying body. She shivered. "God—it's like he's smiling."

Ruby was right. It really did seem as if the general was grinning.

"You're dead," Stoker gasped through clenched lips.

"Not yet," I said as the general's eyes closed for the last time.

Hunter moved forward and reached out to pull at Ruby's arm. "Let's go."

We followed Hunter outside into the night air, stopping for a moment to watch the chaotic scene.

Hundreds of Krails were pouring out of the open main gates. They ignored the officers who ran alongside them, too busy trying to escape to take any notice. But I had no doubt that few of the officers would survive the day. The Krails had never been given any mercy by their captors so I couldn't see them giving any mercy back. Revenge would come later.

"Come on." Hunter ran. We followed.

The Krail leader had only gone a short distance before he keeled over. Concerned, Ruby and I ran up to him.

"Hunter, what is it?" I bent down and pulled his jacket back, revealing a large, gaping red hole in his stomach.

"He's been shot." Ruby looked at Hunter's bloody body.

"Admiring my work," a voice said.

We both spun round. Jake pointed a gun at us.

"What are you doing here, Teerman? Don't you want to escape?" I asked.

"You are such idiots. You could have had everything. Instead, you messed it up for all of us. Sure I want to escape, but first I have to do something I've been meaning to do ever since I met you. And here's the beauty of it: When I pull the trigger, I'll still just be following orders. Adios, douchebag!"

Jake's finger tightened on the pistol's trigger as I charged, expecting at any moment to hear the sound of the gun being fired and a bullet burrowing into my body. Out of the corner of my eye, I glimpsed something glittering pass by me as I barreled into Jake. Together we fell to the ground. I raised my fist, ready to pummel him—incredulous that I was still alive.

"Hogan, he's dead!" Ruby shouted.

"What?"

"He's dead."

I pulled away and looked down at Jake. His eyes were wide open in shock. A large shiny stone was embedded in his forehead.

Getting up, I walked across to Hunter and bent over him. His breathing was shallow, his eyes almost closed. "That Jake fellow wanted those diamonds so badly," he moaned. "I figured…he'd appreciate one more."

"Thank you," I said quietly.

His lips pulled into a small smile as he closed his eyes.

I felt a hand touch my arm. "Come on, Hogan, we've got to go," Ruby said.

"We have to take him."

"He's dying. There's nothing we can do."

"I'm not leaving him."

I reached under Hunter's shoulders and tried to pull him up.

"Please help me, Ruby," I said.

She wound her hand around the big Krail as I pushed my arm under Hunter's bloody body. Straining, we lifted Hunter.

Supporting the Krail leader between us, we stumbled toward the open entrance gates.

"Termination in four minutes. Evacuate! Evacuate now!" the computer ordered.

It was madness. We were going to be the last to leave, and my decision to take Hunter with us meant we probably wouldn't make it out. But I could hear Hunter breathing, and as long as he was still alive, I knew I couldn't leave him.

"Ruby, go," I said as we neared the gates. "You still have time."

"You are the most stubborn man I've ever met, Hogan Duran, but there's no way I'm abandoning you. We're a team. Hunter, you, and me."

I looked across and smiled. Ruby certainly was one helluva woman.

CHAPTER
TWENTY ONE

I<small>T WAS</small> T<small>ABIKA WHO SAVED</small> us. He and a group of bike-riding Krails skidded to a halt as we staggered out of the main gates. They instantly took charge. Three of the Krails took Hunter from us, lifted him into a bike sidecar, and immediately took off.

Tabika yelled for me to climb on the back of his cycle, while Ruby was told to ride pillion on a bike ridden by Wreckage. We accelerated away, following the bike and sidecar carrying Hunter, and wove across the dusty plain.

We'd managed to get a distance from the base before we heard and felt the explosion.

The sky turned red as the blast slammed into us. I held on tight to Tabika's shoulders, my ears ringing as the Krails fought to control their bikes. Ahead, through the curtain of black soot and dust, I glimpsed the sidecar carrying Hunter swerving from to side to side, the Krail using all his skill to stop it from flipping over.

I sneaked a glance behind. Towering yellow flames engulfed the blackened, twisted remains of the fortress. Once the fire had completed its work, I doubted much would be left of NSC Training Base 17.

Tabika turned and gave me the thumbs up. I looked across at Ruby. Clinging tightly to Wreckage, she moved around on her seat and smiled. It had been touch and go for a moment there, but now it looked like Ruby and I were going to make it!

I said a silent prayer that Hunter would be okay, too, but I knew his chances were slim.

The bikes sped on, their bright headlights cutting through the darkness until we finally reached the hills and started to wind along a steep, narrow track. As we climbed, we saw armed men looking down from the cliffs above. They followed the path of our bikes, signaling to one another as we continued our journey.

Eventually the track widened out and the mountain began to plateau. Here the rocks were honeycombed with caves. Women and children looked out at us as we roared past.

Finally, we reached the rock's peak and halted.

Krails rushed across to carefully lift Hunter out of the sidecar and gently carry him into a large cave.

We dismounted and went to follow, but Krails blocked our way.

"Stay here," Tabika said. "Leave us to attend to Hunter."

Over the next few hours, we heard little about Hunter's condition, except that he was barely clinging to life. While we waited, Tabika led us further up the hill to the site of a waterfall and small lake.

Ruby and I ripped off our clothes and dove into the clean spring water. Washing the dust and grime from our bodies felt like ascending to another plane of existence.

Getting out, we were given towels to dry ourselves. Our filthy clothes had been taken away, replaced by Krail leathers.

After dressing, we lay back on the rocks, ate the cheese and bread, and drank the water the Krails had bought us.

Neither of us spoke for a while. We had so much to think about, so much to take in.

"Hogan?" Ruby said finally.

"Yeah?"

"There's one thing that I don't understand. Why couldn't Stoker stop the termination countdown? He knew the code was Level Twenty-one."

"I was thinking about that too, and I think I know the reason. The code was changed daily, right?"

"So?"

"By the time Stoker arrived in the chamber room, it was past midnight. New code. Even he couldn't know it if he hadn't been told."

I had to catch my breath. We'd avoided capture—and sure destruction—by mere seconds.

Tabika returned an hour later. He signaled us to follow him.

"How is Hunter?" I asked as we made our way back down the rocky trail.

"You'll see."

Entering the plateau where we'd first arrived, we saw a huge blazing campfire. All around it hundreds and hundreds of Krails stood silently.

"Tabika, what is this? What's going on?" Ruby asked.

"They are ready to speak to the spirits about our leader, about Hunter."

Tabika raised his hands as the Krails looked on.

"Hunter has led us to many victories." He looked up to the heavens. "Now we are calling on you to give him the strength to win one more battle, the battle for life."

A Krail woman stepped out of the crowd and walked over to join Tabika. She started to sing, her melodic voice echoing around the rocks.

> *Hold on to what is good,*
> *Even if it is a handful of earth.*

The other Krails joined in.

> *Hold on to what you believe,*
> *like the tree that stands alone*

> *Hold on to what you must do,*
> *even when it is a long way from here.*

Hold on to life,
even when it is easier letting go.

Hold on to my hand,
even when I have gone away from you.

We watched transfixed. The song was simple but incredibly moving. When it finished, the Krails stood in silence for a moment before turning to stare at Ruby and me.

"Why are they all looking at us like that?" I whispered to Tabika.

"Because you are not yet Krail. Our strength, our survival depends on unity. You need to take the ceremony. Only with your help can the spirits save Hunter."

As Tabika spoke, the Krails started to chant: "Krail! Krail! Krail!"

"Come with me." Tabika led Ruby and me toward the fire. "You need to undress."

I looked across at Ruby. Both of us had made a decision on the drive up the mountain. Whoever these Krails were, they were not the uneducated, thieving savages we had been led to believe. That was a lie. We knew that now.

Holding hands, Tabika led us naked toward the fire.

"Halt," he said.

We waited as he pushed through the crowd and reached for a branding iron stuck deep into the fire's hot embers.

Krail guards grasped my arms and pinned them behind my back as Tabika returned.

"A true Krail will not call out," Tabika said, his voice booming.

"Turn," he commanded.

I moved my head to the left, exposing my neck. I was unsure what was going to happen, but I knew the Krails meant me no harm.

Wreckage walked over and took the branding iron from Tabika. He pushed it hard against my skin. My face contorted in pain, but I fought back the urge to scream. I glanced down to see a small red eye branded just below my left shoulder—the Mark of the Krail.

Wreckage handed the iron back to Tabika who again pushed it into the fire embers, heating it up for Ruby. Then he pulled the poker out, swung it around, and drove the branding tip into Ruby's shoulder. Despite her obvious pain, she too suppressed her scream.

Tabika pulled the branding iron away and placed it on the ground. He stepped back to stare at us.

"The mark is made!" he shouted.

"The mark is made!" the other Krails echoed.

"Krails!" screamed Tabika.

"Krails! Krails! Krails! Krails!" the others chorused, stamping hard on the rock beneath their feet.

A flash of light lit up the dark sky.

The crowd hushed and turned towards the cave.

I peered through the smoke and flames.

Another bolt of light flashed as a huge naked figure appeared at the cavern entrance.

He raised his hand in victory.

Hunter.

He seemed to stare directly at Ruby and I as he started to speak.

"This is not the end," Hunter thundered. "This... This is just the beginning!"

ABOUT THE AUTHOR

Clive Fleury is an award-winning author and screenwriter, and a TV and film director and producer. He has worked for major broadcasters and studios on a wide variety of successful projects in the US, UK, Australia, Europe, and the Middle East. Clive is British but currently lives in Miami, Florida with his wife and teenage daughter.

CONNECT WITH CLIVE FLEURY

If you would like to know more, please visit:

www.clivefleurywriter.com

Twitter

@CliveFleury

OTHER BOOKS BY CLIVE

Scary Lizzy

The Boy Next Door

Art Pengriffin and The Curse of the Four
by Norman Revill and Clive Fleury

GET BOOK DISCOUNTS AND DEALS

Get discounts and special deals on our bestselling books at

www.TCKpublishing.com/bookdeals

ONE LAST THING...

Thank you for reading! If you enjoyed this book, I'd be very grateful if you'd post a short review on Amazon. I read every comment personally and am always learning how to make this book even better. Your support really does make a difference.

Search for *Kill Code* by Clive Fleury to leave your review.

Thanks again for your support!

www.ingramcontent.com/pod-product-compliance
Lightning Source LLC
Chambersburg PA
CBHW071002120726
47910CB00004B/1343

* 9 7 8 1 6 3 1 6 1 0 5 6 1 *